Treasure in Paradise: The Bolton Chronicles

Book 2: Underwater Passage

By Alan Van Ormer

Copyright © 2023 Alan Van Ormer

Winged Publications

All rights reserved. No part of this publication may be reproduced, stored in a retrieval system, or transmitted in any form or by any means, with the exception of brief quotations in printed reviews.

This book is a work of fiction. The characters in this story are the product of the author's imagination and are completely fictitious.

ISBN-13: 978-1-962168-37-3

Chapter 1

Kelsey Lawrence caught her breath. "Wil, why did you let him into our cabin?"

"What are you talking about?" Wil Bolton asked wiping sweat from his forehead. He surveyed the landscape near his cabin in Nemo, South Dakota, located in the Black Hills. They had raced out of the cabin after three brothers of a man Wil helped arrest arrived looking for revenge. He turned to glance at her.

"I'm saying last night you let Sebastian Peak in, and earlier this morning you allowed his brother to enter."

"For your information, Sebastian broke down the door, and what was I supposed to do with Silas? Why did you hit Silas with the frying pan considering I had everything under control?"

"It worked the last time with the bigger guy, so I thought it would do the same, and believe me, you didn't have anything under control."

Wil gazed at the woman with beautiful green eyes and tousled blondish hair. She'd let her hair grow since the first time he met her two months earlier. He liked it longer. It matched her fiery personality. Wil shook his head.

"Don't shake your head at me. Is this your way of keeping me here in South Dakota? If it is, you're doing a piss poor job."

"What are you talking about?"

"I've been here for two months, and I'm having a hard time deciding whether I should stay or leave. When things like this happen, it makes me wonder."

"How is this relevant to what is happening right now?"

She posted her hands on her hips. "Who doesn't have a door on their bathroom?"

"We fixed it, and now the bathroom is fine. Again, how is any of this relevant?"

"I'm sorry, Wil. I told you I'm scared, and I say and do stupid things when I'm scared."

Wil pulled her close and held her tight.

"I need you to hold me tight." Then she broke free and turned to face him. "What about that?"

Wil switched his eyes to where she was pointing. A black bear was sauntering its way toward them. She started to run. He eyed her. "What are you doing? Stand still and don't move."

The black bear stood there, eying the two, not sure what to think. Then the bear snapped its head at the shouting coming from behind the cabin.

"I think they went this way, Silas."

The bear turned and headed in the direction of the voices.

"Move. Now," Wil said. He took Kelsey's hand, and the two ran as fast as they could. Until he slipped, and the two went sliding down a small hill into Box Elder Creek.

Wiping the boggy water off his hands, Wil glanced

up at her. "Are you okay?"

She huffed out a sarcastic laugh.

"What?"

"Is this how you save people?" She said shaking from the cold water.

He pulled her to her feet, and the two started running once more. Once they were out of the clearing and into the trees, Wil stopped listening to what nature was saying.

"Do you think we've lost them?" Kelsey asked.

"Not a chance."

"How far is the Nemo guest-ranch store?"

"Probably close to a mile."

He took her hand, and they started walking once more. It was thirty minutes before they arrived at the store. "Can we use your phone to call the sheriff? Silas and his brothers broke into our cabin and coming after us." Once he finished the conversation with the county sheriff dispatch, Wil ambled over to Kelsey who sat in a chair in the middle of the store. He pulled up another chair to sit by Kelsey. "Sheriff will be here in a few moments. Actually, there is a car in the vicinity."

She looked around the store. "This is a cute little place with lots of interesting gifts. It's safe."

When Wil noticed her lip was trembling, he reached over and touched her hand. "What's really wrong?"

A tear dribbled down her cheek. "I don't know what to think about any of this. I love you and want to be in your life."

Wil was getting ready to say something when a deputy sheriff walked in. He waved at Wil and Kelsey, then started laughing.

"What?" Wil asked.

"The Peak brothers just ran up to us and asked to be arrested."

"What?" Wil asked. "Are they that stupid?"

"They said a black bear chased them right into the squad car. Two of them climbed into the back seat and locked the door. Funniest thing I ever saw."

Wil shook his head. "Do you need a statement from us?"

The deputy glanced over at Kelsey. "Are you okay?"

Kelsey offered a weak smile. "I'm fine."

Chapter 2

Xavier Holloman stepped off the plane and placed his sunglasses over his eyes. He looked around the capital city of Port Moresby, or as some people called it, Pom City. No time for looking around, Holloman was here for a specific reason for his boss, Hank Lawrence.

As he headed toward the terminal, he thought about Wil Bolton. The guy had found all the listening devices he had planted in the South Dakota cabin, which was unfortunate because his boss had hoped to retrieve information about his daughter's clothing business and about Bolton's treasure group.

On the other hand, finding out another layer of Bolton wasn't all bad. Holloman had found out that Bolton was a formidable foe and one he would have to do a better job of dealing with. For sure, Holloman's ruse of using Kelsey as his daughter hadn't worked out, so he'd have to go a different direction.

For now he was in Papua New Guinea, researching lost airplanes from World War II, specifically a unique piece of debris that could put him and his boss on the map as leading treasure hunters. Bolton had won the first round, but Holloman would make sure Mr.

Lawrence came out on top this round.

Once inside the airport terminal, he scanned the area for his contacts. He finally saw two men who looked like the photos he had seen before he arrived in the Pacific Ocean country.

Xavier hurried over to them.

"Nigel Daniels, Daniel Mark?" he asked softly.

The taller guy nodded. "You must be Holloman."

"I am. What do you have for me?"

"Come this way, and we'll talk at another location."

Holloman joined the two men in a vehicle, and they drove along the coast for fifteen minutes, then they pulled into a grassy area where there stood a bamboo hut on stilts with a leafy type of roof, probably coconut leaf.

Nigel explained. "At times the water can be high along the ocean, so we build our homes on stilts. Please join us in my house."

Holloman followed the two guys up six steps and into the hut. It was a one-room house with everything packed together into one room, including a single bed and a bunk bed.

"We like to live comfortably," Nigel smiled. "Would you like a drink?"

"It is hot here."

Nigel brought out three solo lemonades. "This is one of our most popular drinks," Daniel said. "Please sit."

The three sat down, and Daniel started the conversation. "We've gathered what you have requested. Included are two different maps of the area in question, as well as diving gear. Nigel is an expert at diving, so he'll help you with that."

"There must be some mistake. I don't plan on diving. I'm gathering preliminary information for a group that will join us in a couple of months."

"That is good because April through October is usually the best time to travel here. There aren't that many people around here, and the rain isn't as prevalent as other times of the year," Nigel said. "May through August is a horrible time."

Xavier leaned forward. "I understand that. No one else must know about this."

"No one knows but us two. We have gathered the necessary documents to proceed, but it should be known that another group has also requested permits to look for treasures."

"Do you know who they are?"

"Mr. Loe is the name on the document."

"We should have figured, Boris Loe. Is there anything you can do to make it difficult for them? I will pay more if need be."

Both men smiled. "For money we can do anything you would like."

Holloman returned the smile. "I may like Papua New Guinea, after all."

Chapter 3

It was Tuesday morning and Kelsey was preparing for her weekly Skype conference call with the clothing and design board back in Chicago. She thought about what had transpired in the short time she had been in South Dakota, and she wondered if she had made the right call staying with Wil.

Of course, she was doing the right thing living with the man she loved despite the bears and the intruders. In the two months she had been here, so many dangerous things had happened. Was this what her future would be like?

The ring of her cell phone broke her train of thought. Hank's name appeared.

"Dad, what do you want?"

"Can't I talk to my daughter?"

"I didn't think you wanted anything to do with me because I decided to stay in South Dakota."

"I'm not too excited about it, so I thought maybe I'd try to talk some sense into you so you'd come back home."

"It won't happen. I'm staying right here with Wil."

"You're going to marry the guy?"

"We've not talked about it."

"What about your fiancé?"

"I broke up with him because I don't love him. You'll remember I told you and Mom I'll never marry unless I'm in love. I love Wil, and if we don't get married, I'm okay with that."

Her father was silent. "In order to be a respectable businesswoman, you have to have a husband."

"That's ridiculous. I can provide you with a list of names if you're interested."

Hank was silent.

"No comeback? I'll make it clear for you. Wil is the man I'm in love with."

"What has happened to you, Kelsey? You've changed," her father said in a gruff voice.

"No, I haven't. I don't want to be like you. My siblings and both you and Mom like different partners, and I'm not ever going to be like that. I will marry Wil someday if he'll have me, but if not, he is the only man I'll be with. End of story."

Hank laughed at his daughter. "You're already like your family. What about Coronado? Paris?"

Once her father hung up, Kelsey sat on the bench and stared out at Box Elder Creek, which flowed a hundred yards away from the cabin. Her dad always seemed to tick her off, but he did bring up a good point about the man in Coronado. She would have to tell Wil about that before it came back to bite her. Turning on her laptop, she waited for Gemini to join her. She jumped back at the voice.

"Where are you, Kelsey? I've been trying to get your attention for a few minutes now." Her office administrator, Gemini Jones was on the line.

"Sorry. I'm in another world. What's up?"

"First, what's up with you?"

Kelsey took a deep breath. "I'm having second thoughts about whether I should stay here or move back to Chicago."

"What happened?"

"I've been here two months, and I've had a gun in my face, worried about Wil during a forest fire, found out he was trapped in a cave, and the other night, I hit a guy over the head with a frying pan when he tried to strangle Wil in our cabin. Not to mention the bear."

"You've had a busy month."

Kelsey chuckled. "You could say that."

"I understand that's probably a lot to deal with in a short period of time, but how do you feel about Wil? Could you leave him and come back to Chicago?"

Kelsey didn't hesitate. "I would miss him so much, but this has scared me. I told myself I'd find a way to deal with my fear because Wil's in my heart, but damn, I didn't think it would be this crazy."

"We'll talk later. The board is on its way in. But, Kelsey, I can tell he's the one, so you have to find a way to deal with this."

~

Wil joined Kelsey on a bench on the porch. He laid a small Bronco pizza next to her. Kelsey looked at him. "Thank you for bringing home dinner. I had a hard time today."

He took her hands. "The situation with the Peak brothers has been tough on you. Then you add all the other things that have happened. So I can understand why you would want to fly back to somewhere safe like the south side of Chicago."

Despite the situation, Kelsey had to laugh. "When

you put it that way, what's happened here is safe. I thought about going home because living in the middle of nature is harder than it looks. For the last hour or so, I've sat here thinking about it, and I've come to a decision: This is my home, and this is where I want to be."

Wil reached over and kissed her on the forehead. "How about we finish the pizza and go for a ride?"

"Sounds like a game plan."

Once they were finished with the pizza, Kelsey climbed into the pickup and sat next to Wil. He drove down Nemo Road and connected with Highway 385. An hour later they pulled into Mount Rushmore's parking lot.

"I've always wanted to visit Mount Rushmore. What a surprise," she said.

He held her hand as they walked up to the carved mountain. "Sometimes just appreciating a man-made creation can help me understand what I deal with each day, but it also helps me recognize the significance of history and to learn about the natural and cultural past of the region."

The two walked through the line of flags that led them to the four figures of George Washington, Thomas Jefferson, Theodore Roosevelt, and Abraham Lincoln.

Kelsey relaxed. "It looks so cool with the sun going down and the lights shining on the stars. Wow, the South Dakota flag with blue and yellow colors. I've never seen the flag before."

The two strolled toward a wall that overlooked an amphitheater where people gathered to look at the four statues rising above them in the rocks. Wil jumped up on the wall, grabbed Kelsey's hand, and pulled her up. She grabbed him around the waist and held tight.

"I like this view. Thank you for bringing me here." She held Wil's hand, and the two watched the evening program. A park ranger stood up front and gave an inspirational talk that focused on the presidents, patriotism, and the nation's history. After his talk, they showed a film and the program concluded with the lighting of the memorial.

Kelsey's eyes were transfixed on the lighting ceremony. "Oh my gosh, that is so beautiful, Wil. We'll have to do things like this more often. Not just in South Dakota but around the world. Please, promise me we will."

"I promise." Wil jumped down off the wall and caught Kelsey who fell into his arms. He didn't hesitate to kiss her.

She grinned. "You finally figured it out. The first few times I did this, you just set me down."

"You fell on purpose?"

"Guilty."

Wil wrapped his arm around Kelsey, and the two ambled back to the parking lot. Kelsey peered up at Wil. "Just admit it, you're trying to cheer me up by showing me something cool."

"There's that."

She snuggled into him. "It's working."

Chapter 4

On Wednesday Kelsey was reading the Rio proposal on her laptop when there was a knock on the cabin door. She opened it to see a guy with long hair and a long beard tied with a rubber band standing there. "Can I help you?" she asked.

The guy smiled at her. "Wil asked me to stop by and look at what needs to be done with the cabin. I understand he added a new bathroom, which I suggested to him two years ago."

Kelsey grinned. "He took care of that, and the roof was fixed. We're hoping to turn one of the bedrooms into an office space or add another bedroom."

"Let's take a look."

The two went around the north side of the cabin. "The master bedroom is in a perfect position with it facing the northwest."

Kelsey stared at him. The guy grinned. "Yeah, I get those stares a lot. It stays cooler and darker when the sun sets."

"Understood."

The two walked to the south side of the house where the other bedroom sat. "Now this may be the best place to add another bedroom to the south. I'm not into it, but many who practice feng shui say it promotes positive energy in your bedroom, and it also suggests that sleeping in a particular direction can promote better sleep and overall health. And then there is another study that suggests when your head is toward the south, it aligns with the earth's electromagnetic field, and that may improve sleep quality."

Kelsey smiled. "We wouldn't want to screw up the earth's electromagnetic field, now would we?"

The man laughed. "We wouldn't."

They continued their walk around the cabin. "Let's take a look inside and see what would be best for the office space."

Kelsey opened the door for him, and they walked into the extra bedroom, which he measured as ten-feet-by-twelve feet. "This is plenty large for an office space. You might want to think about pushing the office to the south of this bedroom, which would allow you to add another bedroom to the west in the future."

"What would the cost be to add an additional bedroom or office to the south?"

"Off the top of my head, it would cost between three thousand and five thousand to add an office and closer to five thousand for a new bedroom on the south side."

"What about if we wanted to add a garage?"

"The best direction for a garage would be on the east side of the cabin, and you could connect it through the kitchen area if you wanted."

"And cost?"

"Ten thousand dollars."

"I knew it wouldn't be cheap, but I don't know if we can afford everything at one time."

"You talk to Wil about it, and then you can contact me to let me know what direction you want to take."

"How long would it take to add the office?"

"We could get it closed within a month for sure if not less, then we can work inside which would take another month or two, so my best guess would be to complete the project by November."

"What about internet connection out here?"

The guy rubbed his beard. "I'm not an expert on the internet, but I do know that there are three different types of connections that are available in rural areas. One is cable internet which is faster than DSL and is highly reliable. The drawback is that during peak usage times, the network could become congested and lead to slower speeds."

Kelsey broke up the conversation. "How about we sit down, have a cup of coffee, and continue our conversation?"

"That would be cool."

The two sat down at the table and the man continued. "DSL stands for digital subscriber line, and it uses telephone lines to deliver internet access to homes and businesses. It's slower than cable but is widely available in rural areas." He sipped on his coffee. "Maybe your best bet is satellite internet because you can use a satellite dish to connect to the internet. It is slower than the other two but is available in most rural areas, and I do know a lot of people use it out here." He looked at her. "How are you getting internet service now?"

"I'm just using Wi-Fi, and it's not very good at this point, but it's working."

"I can imagine. Anyway, that lays everything out

for you. Let me know what you want to do."

~

The wedding day had finally arrived for Bailey Blue and Laney Pruitt, two of Wil's best friends. They had settled on having the ceremony at the State Game Lodge in Custer State Park. The ceremony would take place on the Grace Coolidge lawn along the banks of Coolidge Creek. The wedding reception was to be held at the event barn where the wedding party could walk on pavement to the reception.

Kelsey stood with Amanda, who worked with the Black Hills National Forest, as Laney checked her hair for the dozenth time. She smiled at the two gals. "It's finally here, and I'm so excited."

"You look elegant," Kelsey said.

"Thank you. The blue one-shoulder floor-length dress really makes you sparkle."

Kelsey blushed. "Blue is my favorite color."

The other two gals laughed.

"What?" Kelsey asked.

"Is it because Wil has dark blue eyes?"

Kelsey's face flushed. "That is just one of his many adorable qualities."

Laney took a deep breath. "Should we do this thing?"

The three gals hugged, and Laney walked out to meet Wil. She had asked him to walk her down the aisle, and he graciously accepted. Wil and Kelsey exchanged glances. Laney reached up and kissed Wil on the cheek, then winked at Kelsey who stood close by. "She's beautiful, and she loves you. Don't you ever forget that."

Wil squeezed Laney's hand. "Are you ready?"

"I am. Let's do it."

After the ceremony Wil and Kelsey stood in the background watching the two with their opening dance.

"She does look beautiful," Kelsey said.

Wil put his arm around Kelsey. "She may be beautiful, but you're gorgeous."

Kelsey peered up into his eyes. "How about you and I join them on the floor?"

Wil took her hand. "I'd be honored."

Chapter 5

Wil and Kelsey hurried to the gate at the Rapid City Airport waiting to board their plane for a flight to Chicago.

"Are you ready for my staff to grill you?" Kelsey grinned.

Wil rolled his eyes. "It can't be worse than meeting your family."

"No, it's not. They'll adore you."

"How would they even know me?"

She grinned. "Simple. I've told them every sordid detail about the guy I love."

"Everything?"

Kelsey chuckled. "There are a couple of personal things I've kept to myself." She cozied close to him. "It seems whenever I sit next to you all I want to do is snuggle close because it's so comforting."

Just then their boarding number was called. Fifteen minutes after they took their seats, the plane taxied down the runway and ascended into the sky for the two-and-half-hour flight to O'Hare International Airport.

Wil opened up a briefcase with papers and started reading information about Papua New Guinea. He turned to her. "Did you know that New Guinea is the world's third largest island country with more than 478,000 square miles behind Indonesia and Madagascar?"

"I'm always learning something new from you."

He kept reading. "Wow, there are more than eight-hundred languages, and only thirteen percent of the people live in urban areas." Wil continued reading. "Here's something interesting that relates to what we're looking for underwater. The New Guinea campaign was one of the major military campaigns between Japan and the Allies. It is estimated that more than 200,000 Japanese, Australian, and American servicemen died."

"How tragic!" Kelsey said.

"Now here's something related to World War II relics. It says provinces like New Britain, Oro, East Sepik, Sandaun, and Morobe all contain vestiges of fighting during the war. The two areas we'll be looking into are Madang and Rabaul, which are said to be renowned for sunken aircraft and airships." Wil resumed reading. "That's not the only thing out there. We'll be looking for costumes, masks, pottery, and canoes among other things."

Kelsey lifted her head. "What are you mainly looking for?"

"I'm not sure at this point. That's part of what this meeting is about."

"I'm just glad I can spend some time with you," she said snuggling back into his shoulder.

Wil went back to reading until he heard Kelsey's light snore.

It was one-thirty when they arrived in Chicago. Kelsey headed to the car rental counter while Wil grabbed the luggage. Thirty minutes later Wil drove onto Interstate 90 toward the downtown area.

He finally exited onto Lake Shore Drive, and Siri directed them to the Magnificent Mile Hilton.

After the valet took Wil's car, they grabbed their luggage and checked into their rooms. Once they entered their fourth-floor room, Kelsey dropped her bag on the king-sized bed and stared out the window.

"Lake Michigan has always been beautiful."

Wil joined her and placed his arms around her. She peered into his eyes. "This is so cool."

He reached down and kissed her on the forehead. "I love the hot tub. You know what that means?"

She laughed. "I promised I'd give you a massage, and tonight I'll keep my promise."

Wil sat on the hotel bed as Kelsey slipped on her blue strapless dress with matching heels. "Can you please zip me up?"

Wil did as she asked.

She sat down on her bed next to him. "Are you okay?"

"Yeah, I'm doing okay. I'm surprised you're going to your folks' place."

She shifted toward him. "Me too, but I'm sure my father has something up his sleeve."

It was seven-thirty when they arrived at the Lawrence mansion. The butler let them in and hugged Kelsey.

She peered up at him. "What's that all about? You've never done that before, Cleland."

"The staff has missed you. Everyone is back in the pool area."

"Thank you."

Kelsey grabbed Wil's hand and led him to the

backyard. They both stopped when they saw Dr. Regret and his wife along with Mr. Loe and his wife.

"What is going on?" Wil asked.

"I have no clue."

Mr. Loe hurried over to Wil and Kelsey. The short man took a deep breath. "I'm sure you're wondering what is happening here."

Wil sighed. "This is strange."

"I never thought this would happen, but Hank Lawrence and I have been discussing a partnership for our treasure hunting and artifact adventures. It's better to work together than fight over everything."

Kelsey peered at Mr. Loe. "You're making a mistake."

"Why do you say that, Ms. Lawrence?"

"Anytime my father or uncle goes into business with anyone, the other party gets ripped off or pays the penalty for doing business with them. If I were you, I'd think about this, but then again it's not my money."

Mrs. Loe smiled at Kelsey. "How about you join me, and let's meet a couple of people."

Kelsey reached over and kissed Wil. "Be careful. Bears are safer."

~

Mrs. Loe and Kelsey ambled over to the bar, and each grabbed a glass of white wine. The older woman nodded at Kelsey. "You do look nice in your dress."

"Thank you," Kelsey smiled. "As do you."

"There are times when I get so tired of dressing up for these events, but when you're a businessman's wife, it's what you have to do. Although I do enjoy the perks. But you, I'm surprised you've given up this lifestyle."

"Mrs. Loe, it was simple when I found Wil, and I

am in love with him."

"Please call me Leticia. Mrs. Loe makes me seem so old, and I am only twenty-six."

Kelsey stood back stunned. "You're much younger than your husband?"

"Yes, Kelsey. My husband is forty-five, and I'm his second wife. His first wife decided to divorce him because she grew tired of all of this."

"That's too bad."

She took a sip of her wine. "Tell me, why you are so dead set against my husband working with your family?"

"I just know how they operate and they're not always aboveboard with whom they deal. They want nothing to do with Wil, and my father continues to try to talk me out of any relationship with him."

"That's the only reason you don't think my husband should work with your family? Because you don't like the way your father is handling your relationship?"

Kelsey frowned at the gal. "No, that's not it. You'll have to talk to others whom my father and uncle have worked with, because everyone tells me I'm just a Lawrence, and I think just like them."

Leticia studied her. "I don't think you do."

Kelsey didn't say anything but sipped on her drink.

Mrs. Loe continued. "Why are you even here?"

"I've been asking myself that question for the last hour, and I still can't figure out the answer."

Mrs. Loe eyed her. "Maybe you miss this lifestyle more than you think. It is hard to give up all of this luxury."

Kelsey thought about it. "Maybe."

She turned to a familiar voice. Nolan. The last person she wanted to see.

"Kelsey, I hoped to see you. You decided to join us."

Mrs. Loe slipped away. Nolan grabbed her hand and held it. "I've missed you so much."

She pulled her hand away quickly. "We're through, and I mean it."

"Your sister probably didn't receive that memo," Nolan said, nodding.

Kelsey turned and noticed Crystal caressing Wil's face with her fingers. Appalled, she hurried over to the two. "Back off, Crystal," she said.

"What do you mean, little sister?"

"I see what you, Nolan, and our father are trying to do."

Crystal grinned. "I like handsome guys, and Wil sticks out among the others in this room."

Kelsey grabbed Wil's hand and pulled him away from her sister's talons.

"What are you doing?" Wil asked.

She stopped and peered up at Wil. "Did you want her to touch you like that?"

"Of course not, but you didn't have to be so rude about it all."

"Fine, do what you want, and I'll do what I want." Kelsey stormed out of the pool area to the front of the house. She sat down on a bench and stared at the fountain. Five minutes later she looked up when Wil sat down next to her.

"You're not okay, are you?"

She wiped away tears. "No, I'm not, and you don't help matters by being so darn nice about everything."

"What do you want from me?"

She looked at him. "I don't want you even thinking about my sister. You realize how many guys she stole from me? Six of them that I can think of off the top of my head."

"What are you talking about?"

She stared out into the night. "Every guy that I liked, she would find a way to break us up by climbing into bed with him, or telling him I liked someone else, or anything she could to break us up. I didn't care about any of the other guys, but you—I don't want that to happen to you, to us. I am so in love with you, and it'll break my heart if she does it to you."

Wil put his arms around Kelsey, and she quickly snuggled into him. "What is really going on here?"

"I shouldn't be here. We shouldn't be here because my family is trying to manipulate you. I even believe his wife's in on it."

"Do you believe that?"

She snapped her head up to look at him. "Wilton Edgar Bolton, my parents are ruthless, and they will do anything they can to destroy someone. And that's what they're doing here; they're trying to break you and Mr. Loe up. Please, do something about it!"

"What do you want me to do?"

"Talk some sense into him and let him know what is happening."

When Wil didn't answer, Kelsey sighed. "You don't believe me, do you?"

"It's not that. I'm just not sure what to do about it."

She stood up. "Do whatever the hell you want! I'm going back to the hotel."

~

Wil headed back into the party and noticed Mr. Loe talking to Kelsey's father. He walked over.

"Wil, I'm glad you joined us," Hank Lawrence said. "We were just talking about the treasure-hunting opportunities."

Wil sighed. "Did you explain to Mr. Loe why Holloman put listening devices in our cabin?"

Hank's eyes shot up. "I…I have no idea what you're talking about."

"Where is Holloman tonight?"

Hank glared at Wil. "He works for Mr. Loe, so why would he be at this party?"

"You'd think he would be here since his daughter, Kelsey, is here, but then again he just took off without a warning when he had a chance to connect with her."

Wil sipped his drink. "You may be fooling Boris, but we both know you have an alternative reason for all of this. My guess is the reason Holloman isn't here is because he's in Papua New Guinea, gathering info or setting things up for your group to search for whatever treasure is out there."

"You have no idea what you're talking about."

Wil took a deep breath. "Don't I? Mr. Loe sent me some information via email, and guess what? It had been printed out, and I didn't do that. The only people who knew about it were Kelsey and Holloman. Kelsey would never do that, so I'm assuming Holloman printed it, and I also believe he's worked with you from the start." Wil turned to Mr. Loe. "Sir, you can decide how you want to deal with this situation, and any dealings with Mr. Lawrence, but I advise you to make sure you know all the facts and check into what is happening behind the scenes before you work together. Also, it might be wise to ask your wife how she's involved." Wil set down his drink on a tray. "I'm going back to the hotel room, and when you decide what direction you're going, Mr. Loe, please let me know."

Chapter 6

When Wil opened the door to the hotel room, Kelsey was sitting on the side of the bed staring out the window.

She turned to look at him. "I'm so sorry for the way I acted tonight," she said.

He sat on the bed near her. "Do you want to talk about it?"

"As I said when I saw my sister touch your face, it pissed me off because she's always done that to the guys I care about, and I especially don't want anything to happen between the two of us."

He held her hands. "Your sister doesn't interest me at all, but you do, and you always will. Now, Mrs. Loe is another piece of work."

"What do you mean?" Kelsey asked.

"She's in cahoots with your father or maybe your brother, because when I asked her husband to check into what she's up to before he makes a decision, your father's face turned white."

"Wow," Kelsey said. "It's interesting you said that because she asked me why I was even there tonight, and if I missed the lifestyle I had before. To be truthful, it made me start thinking about my previous life, but when I returned to the hotel, I felt like a real jerk because I don't miss it, but I would miss was being with you."

The two were quiet. Kelsey peered up at Wil. "Are they going to work together?"

"I doubt it."

"Why?"

"I asked your dad where Holloman was and pointed out that he still works for him, which Boris Loe and I figured, but your father denied it. Furthermore, I asked him why Holloman stole information from me about Papua New Guinea. The only one who knew about it was you, but then again since he'd planted the listening devices, which I pointed out, he would know about it."

"Holloman actually stole something from you?"

Wil shook his head. "Nope, I made sure any info that I had was sealed tight so he wouldn't know about it."

"You are such a liar! Wait, you knew Holloman was faking?"

"From the start because of our conversation in the caves. The first time he said anything about you, he said he'd been with you since you were sixteen, then the next time he mentioned he had been working with your father for twenty-six years."

Kelsey's eyes shot up to look at Wil. "What does my father hope to gain with this? Hold it, I already know. He's crooked and will do anything to get ahead."

"One last thing. I'm sorry for the way I acted tonight. I don't want you to ever think that I don't care about you or love you, because I always will."

She grinned. "I remember you said you enjoyed

massages. How about we take care of that and more in the hot tub?"

~

Wil and Kelsey drove to her office the next morning. Kelsey wanted him to meet her staff and then Wil would travel to Loe's corporate office along Lake Michigan later in the morning for a luncheon meeting with Loe and others.

A redheaded gal with large glasses spoke. "Kelsey, is this the guy you've been telling everyone about?"

Kelsey nodded. "Wil, meet Gemini Jones, who is probably my closest friend."

Gemini gazed up at Wil. "You are one handsome dude. Kelsey finally got it right. I could tell you about some of the crazy tastes she has in men."

Kelsey blushed. "We don't have to go into any details."

The three laughed. Kelsey showed Wil around the office, including a large room where designers spent most of their time coming up with new drawings for the clothing. He also met the production manager who explained to Wil how everything operated.

"One of the key shifts for twenty-first century office design is a move away from private workspaces to a collaborative workspace," the manager, with short blond hair, explained. "Of course, there is also increased integration of technology." She continued. "As you can see, we have feature rails along the walls so team members can hang and display garments." She pointed to sliding doors along the wall. "We've developed high-density storage solutions that we can modify to house any type of clothing." Opening one of the storage units, she explained, "We have space to store presentation boards throughout the duration of a project."

Wil was impressed. "How do you track items?"

"Good question," the manager said. "We usually apply radio frequency identification chips, more commonly known as RFID, which contain readable information and is attached to a physical object, such as a sweater, for example. This allows the item to be organized into a database for cataloguing."

"Impressive," Wil said. "You also made it easy to understand. Thank you."

She smiled. "You're more than welcome, and we're glad you have an interest in what we're doing. Kelsey had said you care about her work, and it shows with your questions and your attention. So many people come through here for tours and spend more time talking to each other than listening to what we have to say. It's appreciated."

Wil turned to Kelsey. "I should be going because I'm supposed to meet Mr. Loe in an hour or so."

"I have to prepare to meet with the board in a few minutes also. I'll see you back at the hotel." She reached up and kissed him on the cheek. "Good luck."

"This should be interesting."

Chapter 7

Wil arrived at Loe Enterprises fifteen minutes before the scheduled eleven briefing. The administrative assistant was waiting for him when he walked in. "This way please, Mr. Bolton." She smiled.

"Thank you, ma'am."

She opened a door to a conference room where Mr. Loe and four others he had not seen before sat.

Mr. Loe stood. "Please, Wil, join us. I'm glad you could make it."

"I'm happy we're still proceeding with the project."

"No question," Mr. Loe said. He took a deep breath. "What happened last night was a mistake and thank you for pointing it out to me. I'm also dealing with my wife. Today is a new day, and we're moving forward. Let me introduce you to who we have here. In essence, this is the new team I've hired to work with you on our treasure and artifact explorations. All are vetted and hand-picked by myself and others, and whom I trust implicitly."

Wil sipped on his water as Mr. Loe continued.

"First, this is Dr. Alman Richter. He's been working in the archaeology field for the past twenty years. He has a ph. D degree and several other certificates from Harvard University. Dr. Richter has been involved with major finds around the world but never in the Pacific region we're focusing on for this trip." Mr. Loe looked around the room. "Dr. Richter has two research specialists with him who have been in the field for at least two years. Meet Ivory Kitchen and Carly Sanders. Both did their studies at the University of California at Berkeley. Finally, Sage Henry is a renowned historian from Columbia University in New York. She has more than fifteen years' experience in studying Pacific-island history at all levels."

Mr. Loe turned to Wil. "This is Wil Bolton, who is the leader of Treasure Paradise. We have some issues to discuss, then we'll break for lunch, and this evening I hope you all will join us for a social gathering with our spouses and significant others." He hit his speakerphone.

"Yes, Mr. Loe."

"We're ready, Toni."

"I'll be right there."

"Toni is an expert in technology and will help with my slides. I'm not very good at that part."

The group chuckled.

A short gal with long red hair and glasses opened the door. "Nice to meet you all."

Loe began his presentation with some background facts dealing with World War II and the strategic position of New Guinea in the battle for the Pacific. "It happened to be the site of the most fiercely fought battles between the Japanese and Allied forces. The island nation was a base for the Japanese at Rabaul."

A slide popped up showing a group of Australian

fighters. "The Australians suffered heavy casualties and feared being captured by the Japanese either meant torture or death."

He slipped to another slide which showed a photo of the natives in the country. "They treated wounded and helped Australians with food and shelter and carried them back to the Allied lines. At one point the Australians called the New Guineans 'Fuzzy Wuzzy Angels,' and the journalists in that day wrote about their heroism."

The next slide contained one word—*Coastwatchers*. "This is the term for the Australian planters who remained behind after the Japanese occupied parts of the country. Military detachments depended on the group to provide them supplies and also served as guides." He peered at the group. "You may be thinking, what has this to do with what we're trying to accomplish? It's important because we'll be counting on local people as guides. There are a couple who have knowledge of what we're looking for."

"And what are we looking for?" Dr. Richter asked.

The next slide popped up showing a piece of art. "Many believe we're looking for World War II artifacts, and in a sense we are, but more importantly we're searching for Oceanic art. It falls into two major categories — before and after Western contact. There are rock paintings and engravings of the Australian aboriginals estimated to be more than forty-thousand years old and are considered the oldest surviving work of Oceanic art."

Another slide appeared. "Granted, the Pacific Ocean still holds World War II relics and ruins including submerged tanks, warships, and aircraft. Here is a photo of a World War II-era Japanese-type tank that sits submerged only inches beneath the surface of Papua's lagoon."

He clicked the next slide. "The best area to start the search for World War II relics is Rabaul, which as I mentioned earlier, was the base for Japanese forces. At the end of the runway rests a Japanese twin-engine, naval-attack bomber. The waters off Rabaul are large diving sites full of aircraft wrecks."

He took a sip of his drink. "But we're searching for something specific. Masks from around the Sepik River in New Guinea which date back to the late nineteenth century are among the most sought-after objects from that area." Loe took a deep breath. "For example, a ceremonial roof figure from the Sepik region of Papua New Guinea went for twice its estimate."

Another slide appeared. "Many of these masks empower objects such as sacred flutes, canoes, lucky amulets, and even yams. Tribal masks vary in size from a few centimeters to over ten feet tall." He continued. "The masks of the Sepik River region are complex, and as I said earlier, they have different purposes including use in ceremonies and rituals to represent spirits, ancestors, and totems. The masks are normally carved from soft wood, but also are made of clay overlay onto turtle or coconut shells. Few masks are worn over the face."

He surveyed the room. "It's safe to say the Sepik River Basin is a natural wonder and home to rich and ancient cultures which few outsiders ever get to see. There are claims of logging-land grab, police brutality, and even killings. Papua New Guinea is considered the world's largest exporter of tropical round logs." He turned to Wil. "Can you add anything?"

Wil surveyed the group. "The Sepik is the longest river on the island of New Guinea and is the second largest in all of Oceania by discharge volume. The majority of the river flows through the provinces of Sandaun and East Sepik." He took a deep breath. "Landforms include swamplands, tropical rainforests, and mountains. The river system is said to be the largest uncontaminated, freshwater system in the Asia-Pacific region. Are there any questions?"

"What about vaccinations?" one of the research assistants asked.

"Since it's a tropical-island country, it is important to get vaccination against yellow fever, cholera, and malaria. That is being taken care of as we speak. Insect repellant should be used throughout your whole stay, a vaccination against polio is also recommended, and tap water should be avoided."

"Is Papua New Guinea safe?" the other research assistant asked.

"Good question," Wil said. "Violent crime and sexual assault rates are high, and petty theft is also a concern. However, you won't be traveling alone, so that shouldn't be an issue. Papua New Guinea also sits in the 'Ring of Fire' with active volcanoes and frequent earthquakes and tsunamis, so it's important to keep up-to-date with local news reports and social media." Wil ran his fingers through his hair. "One last thing. We'll be heading to Papua sometime in October and hopefully be home by Thanksgiving."

After that, Wil and Loe stayed back to talk. Loe met Wil's eyes. "I wanted to talk to you about last night. I appreciate you pointing out what was happening with Lawrence. Everything you had to say was accurate, and I should have known better because of past experiences with the family." He took a deep breath and peered around the room. "You're the only one who knows exactly what I'm looking for. We are searching for masks, but there is also a treasure hidden in an underwater passage of sorts that no one has ever been able to locate. It's connected with the Sepik River and the Pacific Ocean somehow, but no one is sure how."

"Interesting. How did you find out about it?"

"One of my connections in Papua is a man named Bopau. He's been searching for this passage for at least ten years but has had no luck and has run out of money. I told him we'd help him, and all he asks is credit for the find plus a thirty-percent gratuity to fund his other treasure hunts. If this works out, I plan on him joining the team."

Wil grinned. "I take it Hank Lawrence is thinking you're chasing World War II artifacts?"

Loe chuckled. "He does, and I know Holloman is there finding maps and setting up a search in the Pacific Ocean near the island but not near the Sepik River."

Chapter 8

Kelsey was kicking her feet in the hotel pool when strong arms lifted her out of the pool. Her eyes popped up to Wil who reached down and kissed her on the lips. He sat her back down. She climbed out of the pool and crawled into his lap.

"What's this?" he asked.

Kelsey passionately kissed him. She stopped and gazed into his eyes. "Wow, did I need that."

"Are you okay?"

"Please hold me for a bit?"

"Did your meeting not go as planned?"

She peered up at Wil. "It was wonderful. We'll be working with the group from Brazil, but Santiago has fired the people who were allegedly involved with drugs."

"Are you saying he didn't know about it?"

"Maybe. My company will handle all the shipment and distribution of the clothing, so that'll take care of that issue."

"Then what's the issue?"

She hesitated. "My family. I've been sitting here in the pool and have decided that I'm breaking ties with them. No longer do I want them in my life. Is that wrong?"

Wil shook his head. "After my conversation with Boris, it's probably best for both of us to stay away from them as much as possible."

Her eyes lit up. "I'm sorry. I should have asked you how the meeting went today."

"Like yours it was wonderful. The trip is being planned as we speak, and we know what we'll be looking for. Some kind of mask and treasure located in an underwater passage. We're flying over there in October and should be back by Thanksgiving."

"What, now you're going under the ocean? You had better be careful."

He smiled. "I plan on it. I'll always come back to you because there is so much we have to do together."

She kissed him. "That there is."

~

As Wil and Kelsey stood at the buffet line waiting to go through for their dinner, she waggled her eyebrows. "You are downright attractive with your black tuxedo and bow tie. It's sometimes important to dress with elegance, and you fit that to a tee."

"What about your floor-length gown? Its red color matches my tuxedo perfectly."

Kelsey's mouth dropped. "When did you become a fashion designer?"

He laughed. "Someday I'll marry a fashion design guru and want to have some idea of what you do."

"That is sweet of you."

The two turned to the voice. "I hope you two are enjoying yourselves."

Kelsey grinned. "Mr. Loe, any time I'm with Wil, I enjoy myself."

"I heard your company completed a big deal today."

"We did," she smiled. "Thank you, but I'm surprised you heard about it so quickly."

"My connections are everywhere." His smile was hard to read.

Wil tilted his head. "What is the purpose of this evening?"

"It's a chance to brag about what we're doing with Treasure Paradise. I hope that the team will draw closer together. In fact, here comes Sage and her boyfriend."

"Kelsey Lawrence, is that really you? You've changed so much."

"Sage Henry, it's been two years since the last time we were together."

"At least. This handsome guy is your latest beau?"

Kelsey smiled. "No, Sage, Wil is my last beau. There will be nobody after him."

"That's wonderful news. You've been waiting for a guy to take your heart, and you found him."

"I did. And who is with you?"

"Craig and I have been dating for the last two months."

Everyone greeted each other. Wil whispered to Kelsey. "I'll grab us some food."

"Thanks, sweetheart."

"I'll join him," Craig said. "I'm hungry."

Once the two left, Sage turned to Kelsey. "Where did you find him? He's gorgeous."

Kelsey grinned. "I met him sitting on a bench in Deadwood."

"What?" Sage laughed.

"Just what I said. I came out of a casino in South

Dakota, and he was counting cobblestones on the street, and I was hooked."

"That's not like you to jump in so quickly."

"It's not, but there is something about Wil that I just can't explain. You're right—he has grabbed my heart, and I know I'll never let it go. What do you think of Treasure Paradise?"

"I'm super excited about going to Papua New Guinea and finding these unique masks."

"That does sound exciting."

Sage's face became solemn. "What does your boyfriend have to do with it all?"

"He runs the operation."

"That's what they said, but how did that happen? He's not that old."

Kelsey looked at her. "You'll be just fine with him. He knows what he's doing."

"I hope so because that area of the world gets pretty crazy."

When the two guys came back with dinner, Kelsey smiled at Wil. "It looks good. Thank you."

Another guy and gal joined them. "Dr. Richter, nice to see you again," Wil said. "This is Dr. Richter and his wife, Angela."

"Impressed, you knew that," Dr. Richter said.

Wil blushed. "I love to read. This is my girlfriend, Kelsey, and Ms. Henry's friend, Craig."

"Nice to meet you all," Dr. Richter said. "Mr. Bolton, I was impressed with your knowledge of the area we're heading into. I've never been there, but now I have a good idea of what we're looking at."

"Thanks," Wil said.

"It was important that you mentioned yellow fever,

cholera, and malaria. I recall that it is a concern in that part of the world."

Wil glanced down at Kelsey's hand, which she had grabbed and squeezed. "Mr. Loe will make sure everything is taken care of. He's very thorough."

"That's why I decided to join this group," Dr. Richter said. "And you, Kelsey, what do you do?"

"I own a clothing and design business here in Chicago."

"Very interesting," the doctor's wife said. "I'd love to chat with you about fashion."

Dr. Richter laughed. "My wife enjoys keeping up with the latest trends."

"I'd enjoy that," Kelsey said.

The doctor turned to Sage. "What do you expect out of this trip?"

"Everybody is hoping to find the masks that Mr. Loe is interested in. There's a lot of history involved with those masks. It is true they were sacred, but what many people don't realize is they were also created for amusement."

"Interesting," Dr. Richter said. "Any way you look at it, this will be an exciting adventure."

~

Back at the hotel room, Wil slipped into his swimsuit and climbed into the hot tub. Kelsey joined him a few minutes later.

"The others don't actually know what you're looking for, do they?" she asked.

"Nope. It's because of your father. Boris doesn't want anyone to know about what's happening, at least at the start."

Kelsey slipped over to Wil and climbed on his

knees. "It's not a good thing to keep secrets from the team you're working with. How does that build camaraderie? More importantly, if you don't tell the truth, are they going to trust you?"

"All good points, but it's not my call."

"I'd beg to differ. They're counting on you to bring them back alive, and I want them to bring you back in one piece, so you had better do something about it."

Wil grinned. "You can be forceful when you want to."

She kissed him. "Only when it concerns you. I want you to come back to me every time you leave me." Kelsey moved around. "Move up a little, so I can massage your back." She crawled behind him, wrapped her legs around his stomach, and began kneading his back.

"That really does feel wonderful. Maybe I should just bring you with me everywhere I go."

Kelsey tilted his head up. "Nope, this and more will be waiting for you when you come home. Just come back safely. That's all I want." She batted her eyes. "Now, I hope for something else."

Wil laughed and started to stand up. "Hang on."

Chapter 9

Wil and Kelsey were sitting on the porch in front of the cabin when Tessa and the kids showed up. Maddie opened the car door and dashed over to them.

"Mom, told me not to pester you too much, but what do you have planned for the weekend?"

"We're going camping."

Maddie frowned. "I've never been camping. Why would any civilized ten-year-old want to do that?"

Kelsey grinned. "I'm a civilized girl, and I loved it."

"If that's the case, then I'll love it."

Wil rolled his eyes.

"What, Uncle Wil? If Aunt Kelsey says it's okay, then it's okay."

They all turned to Jonathan who came running over to the three. "I'm ready for whatever we're going to do this weekend."

"We're going camping," Maddie said with her hands on her hips. "I didn't want to at first, but Aunt Kelsey said it was okay, so now we're going to go camping."

"You are, are you?" Tessa asked, walking up to them. "I hope you enjoy yourself. Can I talk to you,

Wil?"

"Sure."

The two walked toward Tessa's car.

"Is everything okay?"

"It is, finally. Our divorce is finalized, and it seems the kids are doing okay."

"It doesn't surprise me," Wil said. "It didn't seem like they had any liking for your ex-husband, which is sad."

"He didn't do anything to cultivate a relationship with the two of them. It was all his oldest son."

"I'm sorry."

"Don't be. I'm just glad it's over. Thank you and Kelsey for watching over the kids this weekend for my exciting trip to Pierre for a banking conference. I guess it was an annual affair, but now they're trying to turn it into every six months."

"You know we love the kids, and they enjoy being with us, so it's no problem."

"You're actually taking them camping?"

"I am. They're going to help set up the campsite, help me start a fire, and grill our meals."

Tessa laughed. "You are the mountain man of the family. They'll enjoy it. I should be back sometime Sunday night."

~

As the group drove toward Blue Bell Lodge in Custer State Park, Maddie was full of questions. "Will the tent sleep all of us?"

Wil peered through the rearview mirror. "It's a four-person tent, so we should be okay."

"What are we going to eat?"

"You and Kelsey are in charge of that."

"I'll have to think about it. What are we going to do?"

"Jonathan and I are in charge of that." He glanced over his shoulder at his nephew. "What do you think?"

Jonathan smiled. "Hiking for sure. Can we ride horses? Can we swim?"

"Count on it. The first thing we're going to do is ride horses before it gets too hot, then we'll hit the lake after lunch."

"Do they have a grocery store?" Maddie asked.

Kelsey jumped in. "They have a convenience store with different varieties of foods, but they also have a restaurant we could try for lunch, if you wish."

Maddie thought about it. "A restaurant would be good for lunch and then grill for supper, if that's okay with you, Uncle Wil?"

"You're the cook."

Maddie turned to her little brother. "Did you hear what he said?"

Jonathan grinned. "I did. Just remember to choose food that I like."

"I'll do that."

It was ten when the four pulled into Blue Bell Lodge. Wil found the parking lot for horseback riding. People were already gathered around waiting for the ten-thirty ride that would last an hour.

Once everyone was saddled, they began the descent up the trail into the Black Hills. Maddie was in front of Wil, and Jonathan was sandwiched between Wil and Kelsey. There were fifteen riders in all including three guides.

The horses had traveled about fifteen minutes when they rode through a grove of trees, and off to the right were a couple of buffalo roaming slowly down another trail. The guides stopped so the tourists could take some photos.

Maddie turned to Wil. "I've only seen a buffalo once, and that was when we went to the zoo, but seeing them out in the wilds is so cool. Thank you, Uncle Wil and Aunt Kelsey."

They continued down the trail and came to the hill that overlooked the valleys both east and west. The guides stopped them once more to allow them to view the landscape. They spent ten minutes looking at the distant Badlands, as well as more of the Black Hills before riding back toward Blue Bell.

After lunch, Wil, Kelsey, and the kids switched into swimming suits and took paddleboat rides. Kelsey and Maddie rode together while Wil and Jonathan were in another boat. They finished the day swimming and roasting marshmallows over a campfire.

By the time it was dark, the two kids started yawning. Wil tucked them into their sleeping bags. He went back out and joined Kelsey who sat close to the fire. He sat down by her and kissed her hand.

"This is so quiet out here. The kids enjoyed their day, and I did too."

"It was fun. Tomorrow we'll take a ride around the Wildlife Loop where they can feed the donkeys and return after lunch. Tessa should be back by then."

"Tell me about the trip you're planning to New Guinea."

"Mr. Loe has all of the paperwork and documents we're going to need, and we'll have to get our shots in the next couple of weeks."

"I had a talk with Gemini on Friday, and she said

that there is a trip planned to Brazil in the middle of October to sign some documents which will make it all official, and the business will spread through the South American region, which is exciting."

"What kind of a contract is it?"

Kelsey finished munching on her marshmallow, then wiped her hands with a napkin. "The major contract is an apparel licensing agreement to manufacture and sell merchandise. We, as the licensor, agree to provide the product and marketing, and in return we receive a percentage of sales the association that comes with a new territory." She continued. "Royalty rates can range from two to twenty percent. We agreed to ten percent of net receipts that we'll receive and are paid on a quarterly basis. And we always have the right to audit the books, which the company does on a regular basis. We could bring in hundreds of thousands of dollars each year depending on what happens."

"What type of clothing are we talking about?"

Kelsey sipped on her drink. "Brazilian fashion has a diverse range of styles, and they feature vibrant colors and tones that include anything from monochrome to tropical and floral prints. Probably some of the larger clothing options are short sundresses, loose-fitting garments, and streetwear like t-shirts, shorts, flip-flops, and sandals."

"It sounds like you have it all figured out."

She smiled. "I continue to progress, and it has been fun."

Wil pulled Kelsey closer to him and wrapped his arms around her. "I'm proud of you and what you've been able to accomplish."

She peered into his eyes and kissed him gently. "You realize you're the first person close to me that has ever told me they're proud of what I've accomplished, and I thank you for that."

Chapter 10

Over the next two weeks, Wil collected everything for his trip to Papua. Tessa had told Kelsey she could stay with them while he was gone, but she politely declined telling her that she would visit from time to time, but she needed to learn how to cope on her own when Wil was gone.

Toward the end of September, Wil sat out on the porch drinking a cup of coffee. Kelsey, who had slept in, finally came out around eight-thirty. Still dressed in her turquoise nightgown with a robe wrapped around her, she carried a cup of coffee.

"I needed this," she said, sitting down next to Wil. She ran her hand through her hair. "I must look like a mess with sleep in my eyes and my hair all knotty."

"You're actually pretty sexy."

She blushed. "You're such a goofball. What are you sitting out here thinking about?"

"How about we go on a hike today?"

"I'd love to. Where to?"

"A place called Sunday Gulch Trail near Sylvan Lake. It is kind of challenging with large boulders and handrails, but the views are wonderful. The four-mile loop offers views of granite and a valley that leads to the northern Black Hills."

"I'll take a shower and make us some breakfast. How does bacon and eggs sound today?"

Wil stared at her.

"What?"

"I'm seeing the domestic side of you, which is pretty cool."

She reached over and kissed his eyelids. "I enjoy it because I love you."

It was ten when the two arrived at Sylvan Lake for their hike along Sunday Gulch Trail. They started their walk along the trail which looped back to Sylvan Lake.

"Wow, look at all the raspberries," Kelsey said, grabbing a handful, sticking one in her mouth, and placing some in a plastic sack in her pocket. She handed Wil a couple which he shoved into his mouth.

"Not bad."

When they came to a small creek crossing, Wil grabbed Kelsey's hand, and the two slowly walked across in order to keep their shoes dry. Wil waited a moment for Kelsey to brush grass off her shoes.

They continued downhill and across some more water. "It seems like there are many water crossings with rocks and bridges," Kelsey said. "It is beautiful out here."

"That it is, but these stairs are steep going down, so be careful."

"I noticed that."

They took a break at the halfway point, found a large rock to sit on, and climbed onto it to view the Black Hills. Kelsey squeezed next to Wil, who placed his arm around her.

He kissed her temple. "This was a good idea. I'd

hoped we would do more of these kinds of trips together."

She pointed to an animal in the distance. "That looks like a sheep or something like that."

"It could be a bighorn, but it's too far away to tell. Let's watch it."

The wild animal strolled toward them and then veered off. Neither could get a good glimpse of the animal. After another thirty minutes, Wil climbed down off the rock, took Kelsey's hand, and helped her down.

The second half of the trip was all uphill, but there were rails to help them hike the trail. They made it back to Sylvan Lake after twelve.

"That was a beautiful trail behind Sylvan Lake," Kelsey said. "I bet there are so many places to hike in the Black Hills."

"There are. What do you want to do for lunch?"

She grinned. "Let's eat a buffalo burger. The first time I was here. I tried one, and it was fairly good."

After lunch, they headed home and arrived at three-thirty.

Kelsey was inside changing her clothes when her cell phone rang. It was her mother calling. "Mom, how are you doing?"

"I'm doing well. Just called to see what you were up to."

"We just got back from an amazing hike up at Sylvan Lake. It was so beautiful, but parts of the hike were difficult because of the uphill climb."

"You're becoming a regular outdoors woman. When are you going to marry your mountain man?"

"We haven't talked about it, but someday we will."

"Are you sure?"

"I'm positive. Right now, we're enjoying our life together, and I'm finding out so much about him, and he's learning who I am. That's important to me."

"What about…you know?"

"Mom, stop. That's none of your business. I'm satisfied with Wil, and that's all I care about." Kelsey finally broke the silence. "Why did you call?"

"We're having a Lawrence reunion and wanted you to be part of it."

"When is it?"

"The weekend after next here at the house. There could be as many as two hundred relatives, many of whom we've never seen before. It should be quite a treat."

"What brought this up, and why such short notice?"

"Crystal and I have been planning it for the past year and thought the first weekend in October was a good time because it is your father's sixtieth birthday."

"I'll talk to Wil about it."

"Why would you have to talk to the mountain man about it? I'm sure he wouldn't be interested in joining us."

Kelsey sighed on her end. "You really don't know how a relationship works, do you? Wil and I talk about everything, and we decide things together. Maybe that's something you and Dad should try?"

"Watch yourself, young lady. I'm still your mother."

Kelsey took a deep breath. "I'll call you back when we've decided. Got to go." She brought a couple of beers out to the porch and sat down by Wil.

He peered up at her. "Your mom or dad?"

She laughed. "Mom, and how would you know that?"

"You always have a beer or two after they call, or you're involved with some maniac who came to the cabin. Is everything okay?"

"They're having a big reunion with a whole lot of family we've never seen before."

"That sounds fun. You should go."

She sipped on her beer and looked at him. "You're not going with me?"

"Depends on when it is."

"The first weekend in October."

"We'll be flying to the South Pacific earlier that week."

She searched the vacant grassland and hills then turned to Wil. "You think I should go?"

"It's your choice, but who knows? You may have fun, or you might find out that the whole Lawrence family is nuts."

She laughed. "That's a good possibility. I hoped you would go with me, but I know you'll be gone by then. I will miss you terribly."

Wil pulled her tight. "I'll miss you also, pretty girl."

Kelsey peered into his eyes. "I hope you don't fall for any of those sexy native girls that dance around with not much on."

"That could be interesting."

She slapped him gently on the arm. "Don't watch too much."

"Kelsey Marie Lawrence, you'll never have to worry about that. You're the only gal I ever think about."

"I know that. Mom asked me when I was going to marry the mountain man. I don't know why everyone associated with me calls you a mountain man, especially after you cut all your hair off."

He drained a swig of beer. "In high school they would call me the 'quiet one,' and I could understand that because I didn't talk much to people."

"I see that. Sometimes it's hard to pry information out of you. Why is that?"

Wil thought for a moment. "Not sure. I've always been shy, and my dad was the one who did all the talking because he always thought everything he had to say was important."

They sat lost in their own thoughts, then Wil broke the silence. "Maddie told me you're not going to stay with them while I'm gone."

Kelsey shook her head because she had just taken a drink of beer. "No, I need to know that I can handle things when you're not around. I'll miss you terribly, but I have to learn to live alone if I'm to live out here when you're gone. Tessa will be there for me as will Amanda and Caleb, if I need anything. I'll be okay."

"Yes, you will. You're much stronger than you give yourself credit for."

"Thanks, but please realize your strength has helped me. I see that, and it makes me realize that everything will be okay no matter what happens. Even if you are trapped under the Pacific Ocean, you'll find a way out because you promised me you'd always come back. I'm holding you to it. Don't disappoint me."

He kissed her. "I promise. Are you hungry?"

"Maybe a bit," she said, crawling on his lap. "Right now, I just want to kiss you."

Chapter 11

Wil and Kelsey waited in the Rapid City airport for their flight to Chicago for different reasons. Wil would be flying to Papua, New Guinea, the next day while Kelsey was going to go to the big Lawrence reunion over the weekend. She had decided to spend a few days at the office, and Gemini and her boyfriend had asked her to stay with them while she was there.

"It begins," Kelsey said. "You'll be gone for at least a month, and I'm not sure how I'm going to handle it."

"You'll be fine. Spend some time with your friends here in Chicago, do some work, and who knows what will happen after that. When are you flying to Australia?"

"Not until after the first of the year."

When they heard their boarding call, they headed onto the plane for the two-and-a-half-hour ride to the Windy City. They settled in as the plane taxied down the runway and bolted into the sky.

"I never get tired of flying," Kelsey said. "How long is it to Port Moresby?"

"Anywhere from eighteen hours to twenty-seven hours depending on where they stop."

"They will have some inflight movies and plenty of food. That I know from my trips to Paris and Budapest."

The two arrived in Chicago at five, grabbed a rental car, and headed to the Hilton Chicago/Magnificent Mile Suites. The Loes were throwing a goodbye party for the group and their spouses that night at their residence.

As they were driving to the party, Kelsey asked, "Didn't Mr. Loe divorce his wife?"

"No, they have worked it out. I don't know how or what happened, but they're still together."

When they arrived, they were escorted to the lower-level area where many people gathered around talking, eating, and drinking.

"I'm glad you two are here," Mrs. Loe said, joining Wil and Kelsey. "Kelsey, I owe you an apology about the way I handled our last meeting. I was way off base about everything I said, and the truth is your father did mention to me that it would be good for you to join his venture. Please accept my apology?"

"It's over with," was all Kelsey said.

Mrs. Loe smiled. "I'm glad that's behind us. Please enjoy yourselves."

Wil and Kelsey strolled over to the buffet and grabbed some food. Kelsey grinned. "What is it with rich people? All they have is shrimp and lobster. Why can't they have hamburgers or hot dogs?"

They both laughed.

"You're becoming a country gal, aren't you?" Wil asked.

Kelsey rolled her eyes. "I didn't ever think that would happen because of the way I was brought up.

You've corrupted me, sweetheart, and I love it."

Dr. Richter and his wife joined them. "Are you ready for the big trip?" he asked Wil.

"I'm looking forward to it. How about you?"

His wife grinned. "My husband's so excited I can't contain him. He's been ready for the past month. Although he got all of his shots six weeks ago, he thought about doing them twice."

They all laughed.

Dr. Richter jumped in. "This is the first real expedition I've had in the Pacific arena and am looking forward to it. I've been reading up on all the customs that are there, and it's fascinating."

"I'm looking forward to it also," Wil said. "But realize that Papua New Guinea is isolated, and from what I've read, it's one of the least explored countries in the world."

Kelsey interrupted. "How has that impacted their cultural life and customs?"

"Good question," Dr. Richter said.

"The country's cultural life and customs have flourished because the outside world hasn't tainted it. Because of the substantial number of tribes living there — some estimate as many as seven-hundred-fifty — there is an abundance of preserved cultures with diverse tribal traditions and ceremonies."

Kelsey grinned. "You've read up on the country."

His wife laughed. "He has spent countless hours researching the area."

Dr. Richter's eyes lit up. "We might be able to join a traditional *mumu* feast where food is wrapped in banana leaves and cooked under stones and also witness a *sing sing*, a performance used as a way for neighboring villages to share their traditions."

His wife grimaced. "You can try that, dear, but I'll stick to lobster."

They all laughed.

"We'll miss the Goroka Show which is in September. That's the biggest festival of the year. However, since we may still be there in November, we can see the Kenu and Kundu Canoe Festival the first week in November."

"Is that something associated with the water?" Kelsey asked.

"It's a cultural event that celebrates traditional sailing canoes and Kundu drums that have been a big part of life in Milne Bay. The canoes and drums were used in rituals to appease the gods. The festival includes dances, canoe races, and war canoes. Briefly it celebrates the coastal people's love of the sea."

They all turned at Mr. Loe's voice. "Are you enjoying yourselves?"

"We're getting a cultural lesson and a list of festivities that Wil will get to experience when he travels next week, and I'm jealous," Kelsey said.

Mr. Loe laughed. "Dr. Richter has been excited about this adventure, and I hope it provides not only a good time for the crew, but also a fruitful one for Treasure Paradise. Wil, can we talk?"

"Sure. I'll be back."

The two walked to another area of the room. "Wil, we've added a nurse and a security guard to the team. Vivian Tusk has been a nurse for the past ten years and is deeply knowledgeable about diseases in tropical countries. Tyler Stamp has just retired from the Marine Corps and will handle security. He's a good friend of the family, so there are no worries there."

"It seems like you have worries about where we're going."

"It's not necessarily where you're traveling to; it's just good to have security to help deal with issues that may come up. He understands completely who's in charge. And we also have our own plane with a pilot and copilot."

"We're going in style," Wil said.

Mr. Loe laughed. "Yes, my concerns are focused on the group's safety, as well as providing all the resources needed to find the artifacts."

"Are we still heading west at nine tomorrow?"

"That's the plan. This is a big expedition, and I hope we can find what we're looking for."

"We'll do what we can to find the artifacts."

"Everything will work out. I should talk to others. Good luck."

Wil found Kelsey with a couple of other ladies and went over to grab a drink. He leaned against a wall and watched the people mingling. An hour later Kelsey joined him.

"Are you okay?"

"Yeah, why do you ask?"

"You've been leaning against this wall for the past hour. Every time I look over here, you look so sad."

"No, not really. I enjoy watching people make fools of themselves when they try to pick up women. How many guys have hit on you?"

Kelsey thought. "At least half a dozen. One of the guys offered to take me around the world."

Wil rolled his eyes. "You didn't take him up on it?"

Kelsey laughed. "Oh, heck no. You'll take me around the world one of these days after you become this rich and famous treasure hunter."

Wil spit out the drink he had been sipping on. "Rich and famous, huh? That's a lot of pressure."

She latched onto his arms. "Are you ready to go back to the hotel?"

"Yeah, I am."

After they returned to their hotel room and fell onto the bed, Kelsey said, "I've decided I'm not going to stay for my family reunion."

Wil turned to face her. "Why not?"

"I want to move forward with my life and not be like everyone else in my family." She sat up and leaned against the bed rail. "I have something I need to tell you, and this is the last piece of dirt you'll hear from me for a while. I'd rather you hear it from me than someone else like my father." She wiped away a tear.

Wil held her tight. "Whatever it is, you can tell me."

She took a deep breath. "Five years ago, I met a guy at one of the design conferences I attend twice a year in Coronado, California. The guy was married, ten years older than I was, and had two children. We had talked about being together."

She wiped another tear away. "Last year, I kissed him, and things were getting heated when there was a knock on the door, and it saved me. The gal at the door had spent time with him also. He had gals in many places, and I was just another one of his flings. My father found out about it and thought I had slept with the guy multiple times over the years."

Kelsey stopped. "Wil, I promise that was as close

as it got. My family has a history of sleeping around, and that night I almost traveled down the same path. I was so disgusted with myself."

She peered into his eyes. "The reason I'm telling you this is to promise there will never be another man in my life. I need you to know that I am not like my family; nor will I ever be because I'm totally in love with you."

Wil pulled her close to him. "I'll never worry about it."

She looked longingly into his eyes. "Please come back safely."

Chapter 12

The next day, Wil and the Treasure Paradise team boarded the plane to Papua, New Guinea. The pilot had told them they would have stopovers in San Diego and Honolulu before reaching Port Moresby in an estimated twenty-three hours. There would be plenty of food and refreshments as well as entertainment.

Wil sat in a back corner of the plane reading more about the Sepik River, specifically about deadly animals that lived there.

He woke up after dreaming about crocodiles as the plane landed in San Diego for a stop.

"We'll be here for two hours while we refuel and pick up some supplies," the captain said. "Please feel free to wander out in the terminal."

Wil and Sage were the only two who took advantage of the layover. The others remained sleeping or reading or talking. The two walked into one of the many souvenir shops in the terminal.

Sage's eyes darted around the shop. "What do you think is the most popular souvenir in San Diego?

Wil thought. "Something to do with a surfboard or a stuffed animal from the zoo."

"That's a good thought," she said, strolling through

the aisles. "A custom-made surfboard is one of the choices, as well as a San Diego-themed t-shirt, a vintage map of the city, a mug with the San Diego skyline, and a bottle of locally made hot sauce." She grinned. "What would be your choice?"

Wil laughed. "It certainly won't be a surfboard because I know nothing about surfing."

"Interesting, you realize that Kelsey has been out here many times and is quite good at surfing."

"I knew she had been in Coronado."

"She's done lots of things you probably don't know about, but then again so have many members of her family, so she fits right in."

Wil changed the subject. "I think I'll buy this mug and the hot sauce to put on our hamburgers."

Sage laughed. "I was thinking of the hot sauce also, but to put it on the seafood back in Chicago. It's kind of crazy because Chicago's known for their deep-dish pizza."

Wil shook his head. "It may just be a Lawrence food they enjoy."

"It could be."

The two boarded the plane for the next stop to Honolulu, after a five-and-a-half-hour flight. Sage sat down next to Wil. "You realize that Papua New Guinea, has a sixteen-hour time difference from Chicago, meaning if it's noon in Chicago, it would be nine the next day."

"Good to know."

She grinned. "I thought you should know so you can time your calls with Kelsey. But of course, once we move out into the wilds, who knows if we'll be able to connect with anyone? Does that bother you?"

"No, it really doesn't."

"Kelsey will worry about what's happening to you, and if she can't find out, it will freak her out."

"She will be just fine."

"I hope so."

Wil looked out the window and then back to her. "You must be ten years older than Kelsey. If so, how did you two meet?"

"You're right, I'm thirty-three, and I met her through her brother, Andy. He and I dated for a short period of time, and Kelsey and I built a bond. She's much different from any member of her family from what I can tell. The others marry for money, and she's always made it known she'd only marry for love."

They both turned when Dr. Richter bought them each a drink. "This lemonade is really good, and I thought you two might want to try it."

Sage sipped the lemonade. "It is surprisingly good. Continuing with my story, Kelsey must really care about you because she's not used to living out in the sticks."

"We make do."

"And you're also very quiet, which is different from most guys she dates who are boisterous and loud."

Wil just waited for her to continue.

"If she's in love with you, you're an extremely fortunate man because her family is very rich."

"Money isn't everything to me. I'm happy with what I do."

"And that's what's strange to me—why Kelsey would even care about you because you're not her type. Granted, you're handsome, but you don't have money and you surely don't dote on her family. I can't figure you out."

"Nothing to figure out other than I'm Wil Bolton."

It was after lunch when they arrived in Honolulu. Wil grabbed himself a sandwich and a drink in one of the restaurants and called Kelsey. It was six p.m. her time. She answered after a couple of rings.

"I hope I'm not bothering you."

"We're just getting ready to eat supper. I'll call you back in an hour. Will that be okay?"

"Yeah, we're scheduled to be in Honolulu for a couple of more hours. And it is beautiful here."

"It sure is. I've been there a couple of times. Talk to you soon."

While waiting, Wil took a tour of Pearl Harbor National Monument. He toured the visitor's center, watched a short film, and explored exhibits that showed what happened on December 7, 1941.

"It was tragic," an older man said to Wil.

"It was," Wil said. "Do you know a lot about it?"

The man nodded. "My father was stationed here when the Japanese hit. He was fortunate that he survived, but he saw many of the more than one-thousand sailors and Marines who lost their lives on the ship during the attack."

"This is the first time I've ever been here, but if I ever come to Honolulu again, this will be a for-sure stop."

"It is for many people who visit Honolulu — veterans and civilians. It draws almost two million visitors each year." He looked at Wil. "Do you wanna walk with me?"

Wil joined him.

"The structure we're on spans the mid-portion of

the sunken battleship and consists of the entry room, the assembly room, and the shrine room."

The two walked into the shrine room. The old man stopped. "Look at the marble wall with the names of those killed engraved on it." He wiped away a tear. "The thing that hits me the most is the words on the plaque: '*The USS Arizona* Memorial is a powerful symbol of resilience that resonates with visitors of all backgrounds.'"

An hour later, Wil was on the boat back to Honolulu when Kelsey called.

"We had a wonderful meal tonight. Gemini cooked some spaghetti and meatballs, one of my favorites."

"I'm glad."

"How is the trip going?"

"It's been interesting. Seeing the *USS Arizona* memorial is something I've always wanted to see, and chatting with Sage has been quite a treat. I didn't know you were a surfer."

"I've been surfing a few times before. Is that a problem?"

"No, it's just something that you never told me about."

There was an uncomfortable silence on the other end. "I didn't think I would have to tell you everything that I've done in my life. Have you told me everything?"

"No."

"That's what I love about you. You're not a guy who pries into my background."

Chapter 13

The group continued their journey to Port Moresby International Airport or also known as Jacksons International Airport. They would spend the night there before heading to Wewak where the expedition would begin.

It was right after lunch when they arrived in Port Moresby. Once the group checked into the hotel, Wil called an all-hands meeting to discuss the Port Moresby area.

"Remember about safety around the city, and if you plan on visiting things, it would be good to do it with others and try to find guides. For instance, I plan on seeing the Varirata National Park and Sirinumu Dam if others are interested in joining me."

Several said they would join him. The others planned to stay in the hotel and get some rest.

After the meeting, Wil contacted Bopau who said he would be over to join him within a half hour.

Ivory, Carly, and Sage waited in the lobby with Wil for Bopau to show up. They had all grabbed some water and snacks for the afternoon.

Carly sat down next to Wil. "This is exciting. I've never done anything like this," she said. "Sage told us you're dating Kelsey Lawrence?"

Wil eyed her. "You could say that. How do you know her?"

"Everybody in Chicago knows the Lawrences. They've made a lot of money over the years and Kelsey runs her own business. She does a wonderful job, and women in the city are proud of what she's accomplished on the business front, but they're not happy about who she is outside of the business world."

They both looked up when Bopau hurried in. "Mr. Wil, it's so good to see you," the little man who stood five-six said, sticking out his hand. "Are you ready for the first trip?"

He nodded. "I have others who will join us."

"Let's go, but remember we need to be careful even during the day. It's a good thing women have guys with them because it is dangerous for them on their own."

"We've heard that," Wil said.

Bopau led them to his Jeep. Once they climbed in, he started down the road. "It's an hour from the city, and there are some sites along the way that are beautiful. Varirata National Park is the county's first national park and has six hiking trails. The longest takes three hours to complete. There are also lookouts with panoramic views of Port Moresby and its vicinity."

Sage jumped in. "Is it safe?"

Bopau nodded. "It is during the day, and you have three capable men with you, me included," he smiled. He led the group down a trail and stopped fifteen minutes into the hike at one of the sites. They stood on top of one of the hills and looked down at a waterfall.

"That's beautiful," Sage said, standing next to Wil.

She pulled out her cell phone and took photos. "How about we take a group photo?"

Another couple walked by, and Sage asked them to take a photo of them together. Afterward, Bopau led them down the trail. They crossed over small foot bridges and walked through little creeks of water.

After about an hour of hiking, Bopau gave them a break. Carly sat down by Wil. "I never thought research would be this hard."

Wil laughed. "I didn't think it would be this hard either. What made you decide to join this group?"

"I worked with Mr. Loe in the past on some projects, and he called me in to talk to me about joining the Treasure Paradise, and I was both flattered and excited. At twenty-three this is a wonderful opportunity to start my career."

"I'm twenty-three. Everyone has told me I'm awfully young to lead a group of this magnitude on a search. I'm fortunate, I guess."

"I wouldn't say that. Mr. Loe and the Lawrences have known each other for many years, and once Kelsey came to South Dakota, it was a given you'd join the group."

Wil stared at her. "What?"

"Mr. Loe and Mr. Lawrence had worked together on this project at the start, and Kelsey joined a group of people who traveled to South Dakota on a trip. Kelsey was in South Dakota for one reason, and that was to find a certain guy who made a living tracking down people and animals. I didn't know who it was, but I assume you were that man."

Bopau had them moving once more. Along the trail they were able to see the ocean, as well as the mountains and trees that dotted the landscape.

Ivory who walked with Carly right behind Sage and Wil commented on the beauty that they witnessed. "Nothing like this in Chicago."

Carly agreed. "There are a couple of nice parks there, but you're right. This is gorgeous."

As they made their way back to where they started, Bopau stopped at a house that looked like it was floating on the water.

Bopau explained, "Many people believe the bamboo house floats on water, but it's built on stilts out of the water. It protects the family from flooding during the rainy season. Many houses are like this in the country. We are almost back to the entrance. Before we go back, I would like to show you the Sirinumu Dam and the artificially-made lake that attracts many visitors. And if we have time, we can visit a local village and interact with indigenous people who live there."

They walked across the dam and stopped to take photos of the lake. As they took photos, Bopau explained that the dam was created by the damming of the Upper Laloki River in 1963. "Water runs to a hydroelectric plant and also supplies water for the city of Port Moresby. As you can see, there are many activities on the lake including boating, fishing, water sports, bird watching, and hiking."

They continued down the trail. Thirty minutes later they arrived in a small village.

"This is one of the many Motu tribes in Papua New Guinea," Bopau said. "The Motu and the Koitabu people are the original inhabitants and owners of the land on which Port Moresby stands. Papua New Guinea has several thousand separate communities, and most of them have only a few hundred people."

Members of the tribe greeted them and escorted them into the village center where what Wil believed was the leader of the village. Bopau translated that the leader had asked them to join them at the center circle where a fire was burning.

"They are preparing for their evening meal. Many of their meals consist of a variety of fruits like pawpaws, pineapples, passion fruit, and mangoes that they mix with their other food."

The group gathered around the fire, and the leader started talking in his native language which Bopau interpreted.

"Many of our population live in rural villages, and our daily life centers on the extended family with the main purpose of producing food and raising children."

The group watched the Motu women cooking in large pots, and others brought out water jars and food platters. Bopau spoke up, "Notice they're elegant but plain."

Sage questioned Bopau, "Do the Motu women have tattoos on their bodies?"

"Traditionally, Motu women wore elaborate tattoos, but the practice has stopped. Music and dance celebrations are still important to the Motu. They mark notable events such as birth, death, peacemaking, and religious observances with music and dance."

Over the next hour, they all sat around and ate a meal. After dinner, a group of dancers started. Again, Bopau translated what the leader was saying.

"They achieve spectacular artistic expression with elaborate feather headdresses, brightly painted faces, arm shells, and plaited amulets. The women wear colorful grass skirts and the men perineal bands."

"Look at the way they dance," Carly said. 'It's almost like they're in a formation."

Bopau nodded. "They dance in different formations to the percussive rhythms of the drums." He swayed to the music and then pointed to the drums. "That is a Kundu drum, which is a type of hourglass-shaped drum that is played with their hands."

He pointed to another drum. "That is a Garamut drum, which is a slit drum that is carved from a single piece of wood and is played by striking the top of the drum with a mallet or stick."

They noticed a third drum, a hand-held one, played with their hands.

"What is that one?" Ivory asked.

"It is the Tifa drum. It is used in dance performances and other festive occasions."

An hour later, they thanked the leader, then Wil and the others made their way out of the village back toward the hotel where they would spend the night. Wil went to his hotel room and crashed immediately.

Chapter 14

Kelsey glanced down at her cell phone. Why hadn't Wil responded? She took a deep breath knowing she'd have to get used to the fact that Wil would be in areas where he couldn't contact her. She sent him a text message.

Hey, sweetheart, I hope you're doing okay. I wanted to let you know I'm hanging in there, but I do miss you and love you, but of course you already know that. We should be flying to Brazil in the next couple of weeks to finalize the contract. Be careful and I love you. Kelsey.

She sat down on the side of the bed in her hotel room. Kelsey had thought about flying back to South Dakota and staying in the cabin until the trip to Brazil in a couple of weeks. She took a deep breath and reminded herself that this would be her and Wil's life for the next couple years, and she'd told him she'd be there for him. And she would.

The next morning, she woke early and decided to go for a run. It was time to get back into exercise, something she'd enjoyed in the past. As she ran with headphones blasting her favorite songs, she thought about nothing but the music and the two miles she had planned on running.

When she arrived back at the hotel and took a walk around the parking lot to cool down, she looked up to see Holloman. "What do you want?" she asked.

"Your father wants to talk to you. He has a proposition for you."

"I have nothing to say to him, so please leave me alone."

"I don't think so. He needs information about what your boyfriend is doing."

Kelsey glared at Holloman. "And I told him I'm through with my family. I'm committed to my life with Wil. For the second time, please leave me alone." She put her hands on her hips and walked away from the guy. After what he pulled in South Dakota claiming to be her father, she wanted nothing to do with him. And for sure she would disconnect any ties with her father and mother. Kelsey entered her hotel room, dropped onto the bed, and stared up at the ceiling. She was out of shape. Her cell phone vibrated, making her jump.

"Wil, is that you?"

"Yes, I received your text and am sorry I haven't been able to contact you. I finally reached a location where I could call you. Are you okay?"

"Yes, I am trying to wrap myself around all that is happening with us. I will be strong and figure out a way to persevere while you're gone. I thought about flying back to South Dakota until we fly to Brazil in a couple of weeks but then chastised myself for being a wimp."

"I don't think you're a wimp. This is new for both of us. I miss you already."

"Glad to hear that. I just got back from a run, and Holloman was waiting for me, wanting information about what you were doing." When he didn't respond, she said, "Wil, I have to tell you the truth. My father wanted me to use you to gather information on what is happening with Treasure Paradise. I haven't said anything."

"Is that why you met me in Deadwood?"

She had trouble finding the words at first. "It started out that way, but I never got that far because I fell in love with you. and that part is true."

"I should probably get off here because the plane is fueled and ready to fly to Wewak, a small town near the river we'll be floating down."

"Please, Wil, be careful. I love you and will be here for you." Kelsey took a deep breath. She had blown it by not telling Wil what she was up to at the start. Now she had no idea what would happen.

~

The plane started its two-hour flight to Wewak. Wil took a window seat and stared out at the Pacific Ocean.

"Is everything okay?" Carly asked, sitting down next to him.

"Yeah, I'm just contemplating what will be happening within the next few days or even months."

"This is going to be a wonderful experience. Have you heard from Kelsey?"

Wil nodded. "Just busy running her clothing and design business. What did you mean about Kelsey searching for a specific guy in South Dakota?"

"Dr. Richter had mentioned Hank Lawrence wanted to find this guy in South Dakota who knew how to stay alive and could find things. I didn't know it was you, but you may be the one they were talking about."

"How would they know anything about me?"

She looked at him. "These guys are rich, and they know everything. Ben Lawrence is a good friend of one of the forest service managers. Sage would know more about what's happening because she and Kelsey have been best friends for more than ten years. She used to work for her father before she moved over to Mr. Loe."

Wil frowned at Carly. "How can you know so much at such a young age?"

She grinned. "I listen."

It was around lunchtime when the plane landed in Wewak. The group headed to the Wewak Boutique Hotel. The rooms were ready for them, and the desk manager handed out keys as they walked in.

Wil and Bopau were down eating lunch when Sage and Dr. Richter joined them. "What are we ordering to eat?"

Bopau smiled. "I talked Wil into eating one of our notable dishes. He chose *Mumu*."

Dr. Richter smiled. "Ah, the national dish of the country. Is it still composed of pork, sweet potato, rice, and vegetables?"

"It is," Bopau nodded. "It is an example of a balanced dish composed of crops and meat, cooked over an earthen oven."

Wil grinned. "I also chose kava to drink, which is a popular, non-alcoholic beverage. Didn't need coffee right now."

Dr. Richter and Sage pored over the menu.

Dr. Richter chose *Kokoda*, a dish consisting of fish cooked in a lime-coconut sauce.

"I'm going with a chicken pot, which consists of chicken stewed with mixed vegetables and coconut cream. I'm also going for kava," Sage said.

As they waited for their meal, Sage started a conversation. "Tomorrow we'll start our quest to find the masks of Papua New Guinea. I'm excited."

Dr. Richter agreed. "It won't be easy because of all the perils we'll encounter along the way, but I'm confident we'll make it through."

Bopau peered at him. "Dr. Richter, don't be fooled about any of this. I've been looking for these items for many years, and it is difficult. The first difficulty will start with the crocodile men of the Sepik region. They believe they control the region, and that will be our first hurdle."

That night most of the group sat around the pool area. Some swam while others were lounged in deck chairs drinking a few beers. Wil stood out on the deck and stared at the ocean waves beating against the sand.

"Despite what may come tomorrow, this is beautiful."

Wil glanced at Vivian who had come out and stood next to him. She had been swimming but covered her bathing suit with a t-shirt.

"I agree with that statement," Wil said.

"Are you worried about the trip?"

"I don't know if I'm worried, but I do know I'll be cautious when we're out there. The river itself is 712 miles long, so we have no idea where to start. But we do know it flows into the Bismarck Sea." He took a deep breath. "The Bismarck Archipelago extends round to the east and the north of the sea, and that encloses the Bismarck Sea and separates it from the Pacific Ocean. If I had to guess, that is where we're going to find what we're looking for."

"Then why are we starting at Kanganum?"

"That's where people say these masks are located. Right now, I'm going to get some sleep. We'll be up early tomorrow."

Chapter 15

Two Jeeps took the group to the starting point of Kanganum on the Sepik River. They arrived at a village along the Sepik River in a little over two hours. Bopau spoke to one of the men in their own language. All he did was nod.

Bopau waved for Wil and the others to follow.

"Look at that," Carly said, standing next to Wil.

Dr. Richter joined them. "Men of the crocodile clan are scarified to look like reptiles. Circles of scar tissue surround the nipples mimicking crocodile eyes and nostrils carved near the abdomen. And if you look at the ones with their backs to us, they're scarred in the form of the animal's rear legs and tail. Magnificent."

Carly looked at the doctor. "Weird, if you ask me."

The doctor frowned. "Don't let anyone hear you say that."

Bopau joined them. "The doctor is correct. Most don't speak English, but some do, and if they heard that comment, we'd be in big trouble. Ma'am, their skins resemble the hide of a crocodile because it is an animal that people in this province believe symbolizes strength, power, and manhood." He turned to Wil. "On another note, they have houses for us to stay in. The gals will stay in one hut and the guys in the other."

The group walked toward the village and noticed most of the huts had simple rooms with bamboo floors, woven walls, and roofs.

"They're up on stilts to protect against river floods," Dr. Richter said.

That afternoon the group learned about everyday life. Some watched as the natives painted their bodies, worked on outfits, played music, danced, and sang. After the evening meal, Wil and Dr. Richter were invited to the Spirit House.

Bopau explained that local women and young men who weren't initiated were not allowed inside. "We can enter, as long as we take off our hats and don't touch anything without checking." Bopau pointed. "Whatever you do, don't touch the decorated crocodile skull. See the shells? They are central to this culture and were once used as currency. They believe this skull has financial worth as well as artistic and spiritual value."

They sat down with the elders and others in the spirit house. One elder started speaking, and Bopau translated. "He wants to know if you have questions."

Dr. Richter asked a question. "What is the purpose of the spirit house?"

Bopau translated his question to the elder who responded. Bopau turned to Dr. Richter. "This structure is used for religious and cultural purposes."

Wil jumped in. "Who built them? And what is the purpose of the artwork and decorations?"

Bopau relayed the message to the elder. He answered the question. Bopau replied. "Men have built these sacred spaces where spirits reside. The decorations and artwork depict the culture and beliefs of the people who built them."

Bopau chatted with them for a few minutes more. He turned to Wil and Dr. Richter. "He has said he will allow two of his men to lead us down the river to the next stop, which is Kambaramba. He knows of two spots which would be a good location to look for the treasures."

Dr. Richter smiled. "That's what we're talking about."

Chapter 16

Everyone was up early the next morning and ready for the trip up the river. The villagers kept one canoe empty for storage of scuba-diving equipment. Bopau had told them they were looking for old relics along the water. The guides were excited about it and were thrilled to help them.

The voyage began, and throughout most of the first day, it was slow going because of the numerous crocodiles floating around. The villagers did more praying to the crocodiles than rowing. Finally, they reached their first night camp.

Wil, Bopau, and Sage sat around the campfire talking about the day. The others had crashed for the night because of the grueling hours of paddling and the heat they encountered along the river.

"Where are we going to search tomorrow?" Wil asked.

"There is a spot about half a day from here that would be a good place to start. I haven't had the chance to go there," Bopau said.

"That's where we'll start. I believe we have only an hour's worth of oxygen underwater. We're going to have to find a couple of more scuba tanks for Dr.

Richter and either Carly or Sage to join us."

"Carly would be the better option," Sage said. "I've never done it before."

"Then Carly it is."

"What do you hope to find?" Sage asked.

"Some special kind of mask that is linked to an ancient civilization. Dr. Richter has all the information on what mask he's looking for."

"I thought you knew about all of this," Sage said.

Wil stared at her. "Where did you get that idea? Dr. Richter is the expert archaeologist. I'm just a guide of sorts."

Sage frowned. "I got it all wrong then."

"Yeah, there are a lot of things that are wrong here, and I hope we make it through okay. I'm going to bed."

Sage grinned. "I could always join you."

"What about your boyfriend?"

She eyed him. "What about him? Isn't Kelsey still your girlfriend?"

~

The group had traveled for a couple of hours when Bopau said they'd reached the spot to dive. Bopau and Wil put on their equipment, dropped over the side, and went down into the river. The water was fairly clear, and they didn't have a bad time seeing things.

"Wil, let's head toward those rocks," Bopau said via the communication system within the scuba gear.

"Lead the way."

It took ten minutes to reach the spot. They looked around for another ten minutes before Wil found something of value. He placed his hand underneath a rock, lifted it, and there sat a little bag. He lifted it out and placed it in a holder the two had carried.

Wil turned when Bopau said something he couldn't understand at first, but then he realized a crocodile was swimming toward them. They scooted up to the surface and made it into the canoe just as the crocodile rose out of the river.

The natives were in a frenzy doing their prayers or whatever it was that they did when they saw a crocodile. As they chanted, the crocodile swam away.

"Did we find anything?" Dr. Richter asked.

Wil kept his eyes on the crocodile. "I'm not sure. We'll see when we arrive at camp."

They found a place to camp after two hours of rowing, set up their tents, and cooked food around a firepit.

"Let's see what you found," Carly said.

Wil opened the bag and pulled out a wooden statue.

Dr. Richter looked at it. "It's Oceanic art; that's for sure. It looks like some kind of ceremonial figure."

"What is it?" Carly asked.

Dr. Richter examined it. "It may be a Telum figure, which is a small devotional image carved from wood. They used them in private rather than communal worship in primitive societies."

"Is it worth anything?" Ivory asked.

"It could be worth a lot," Dr. Richter said. "We'll see when this is all finished."

Several crawled into their sleeping bags while others sat around the campfire talking about the day.

"The river is so cool," Carly said. "I've never seen so many crocodiles in one place."

Sage shook her head. "This is fascinating, but it's also kind of scary."

Wil looked around the area. "Tomorrow is another day, and we'll see what happens."

Dr. Richter jumped in. "I have a great feeling about tomorrow. Finding a ceremonial figure was a good start. It can only improve from there. We're going to find some important items."

Over the next thirty minutes, people went to their tents. Wil and Carly were the only ones left.

"Sorry about our earlier conversations. I said things I shouldn't have, and I've been fretting about it ever since."

"Don't worry. Sometimes it just doesn't work out."

Carly sighed. "Don't I know. I dated a guy for two years only to find out he had not just one, but two girlfriends. You'd think I would have figured it out."

"That's crappy."

"It is, but it just makes me more careful."

Wil changed the subject. "I want you to dive with us on our next dive."

"Wow I'm game. I thought it would have been Sage because she loves diving. Sage, Kelsey, her brother, Andy, and Nolan, Kelsey's boyfriend always dived together."

"Nope. You'll have your chance tomorrow."

Carly stood. "I'm heading to bed. See you tomorrow."

"Good night."

Wil stared into the fire. So many things just didn't add up. Who could he trust?

Chapter 17

The group was up early, ate breakfast, and was on the river by eight. The destination was Kambaramba. They rowed for about ninety minutes when Bopau suggested they stop and check out one place. This time Carly put on the scuba equipment along with Wil. They would pick up more equipment in Kambaramba.

"Be very careful down there, Wil," Bopau said. "There are freshwater sharks that roam in this area."

"Will do."

Wil and Carly rolled back into the river and dove down toward the bottom. "Is your communication system working?" Wil asked.

"It is," Carly said.

The two swam toward an area where there were a group of rocks. Carly stopped and pointed at something shining. "What is that, Wil?"

"I don't know, but let's take a closer look." Wil hurried over to the location Carly pointed at. He did a little digging and found a pistol. "Is that Japanese made?" Carly asked.

"It sure looks like it, and it seems to be in good condition." Wil retrieved the pistol and put it into his pack. The two continued skimming along the ground for anything else. Carly found a medal of some sorts.

"It has gold leaves and some type of flower and looks like a radiant sun," Carly said. She stuck it into her pack, and they continued floating along the river floor.

Fifteen minutes later, Wil spoke. "We had better head up to the top."

It took them another ten minutes to make it to the surface. They climbed onboard where the crew waited for them.

"What did you find?" Dr. Richter asked.

"A couple of things," Wil said. "A Japanese pistol of some kind, and Carly found a medal."

She pulled it out and showed it to the others.

"Wow," Dr. Richter said. "That medal is called 'The Order of the Rising Sun.' It is the first national decoration awarded by the Japanese government back in the late 1800s. Prior to the end of World War II, it was awarded for exemplary military service."

Carly pointed at the filagree. "What type of flower is that?"

"It's a paulonia flower which is the blossom of a Japanese ornamental tree. The medal itself depicts a radiant sun suspended from a paulonia leaf and blossom."

Wil could tell the professor was in his element.

"Let's see the pistol." Dr. Richter said.

Wil pulled it out and handed it to Dr. Richter.

He studied it. "This is a Japanese-issued Type 26, nine-millimeter Nambu revolver that was usually issued to noncommissioned officers during World War II." He examined the pistol closely. "It is a semi-automatic pistol, and it looks like it still could be in good condition."

Bopau interrupted. "Maybe we should go to Kambaramba before it gets dark."

They loaded onto the canoes and made their way to the village. By the time they arrived, it was dark except for the native fires burning to light the way. Bopau was the first one off and talked to a couple villagers who stood waiting for them.

He turned back to the group. "They wait for us."

They unloaded and made their way to different huts which looked the same as the last village's huts. Their group joined the villagers for supper, but right after the meal, many went straight to their huts and slept. Wil, Bopau, and Carly stayed with the natives and talked to them.

Wil looked over at Bopau. "Ask them if they know anything about the Bismarck Sea." Bopau relayed his message and listened as the elder spoke.

He turned to Wil. "He said it's a two-day journey from here, but it can be very dangerous this time of the year because of heavy winds, rain, and at times typhoons will hit."

"Has anyone from his tribe ever been there?"

Bopau asked him the question. The man shook his head and spoke. Bopau turned to Wil. "They don't go there because the natives are afraid. He won't say about what, but there is an area of the river that is deep, and many people don't come back if they fall in it."

The next morning the group made its way to Angoram. Toward midafternoon they came closer to the town and noticed various plantations around the river.

"Are those rubber and cocoa plantations?" Ivory asked.

Sage nodded. "We're in a more civilized area right now."

Bopau pointed out the stilts on which the huts stood along the river. They pulled into a dock and climbed off the canoes to many people greeting them.

Bopau spoke to them. "They are glad to see us and ask that we make ourselves comfortable," he told the others.

Wil turned and noticed a small cruise boat sailing by them and people waving at them from onboard.

Bopau explained, "Many groups set up tours along the Sepik River. It is the best way to travel along the river."

They decided to set up camp outside the village. Once finished, they joined the villagers to watch how they did things.

Sage pointed. "Another one of those spirit houses."

Bopau nodded. "Most villages are animists. It's particularly important to them."

Wil noticed the security guard, Stamp, always staying close to Sage. Ivory stood next to Wil. "I see you notice that Ms. Henry and Mr. Stamp are becoming cozy."

"That's their concern," Wil said.

Ivory sighed. "True, I've tried to cozy up to Carly, but she seems to rebuff my advances."

"Again, I can't answer that."

Ivory grinned. "I'm sure it's because she's interested in you. She's a good catch."

Wil shook his head as he walked away. He glanced down as his cell phone vibrated.

"Hello."

It was his sister, Tessa. "You are alive!"

"Yeah, why wouldn't I be?"

"Good point. How are things going?"

"It's been an adventure. How are the kids doing?"

"Maddie is especially missing you."

"Tell her I miss her also."

"Have you called Kelsey?"

"I talked to her the other night, but I wonder if I've been used by her and her family."

"Why would you say that?"

"Just some things that have been said on this trip."

"Don't believe everything you hear, little brother. Trust Kelsey."

"Maybe you're right."

She continued. "On another strange note, I actually heard from Del over the weekend. He hasn't called me in years. He said he and his wife plan to be in the area in a couple of weeks. Did you even know he was married?"

"Nope. You know more about him than I ever would."

"They live in Wyoming with Grandpa and Grandma in the Bighorn Mountains."

Wil laughed. "Family drama. We have found some remarkable items here in the last week. A couple of days ago, we found a wooden figurine and yesterday Carly found an old Japanese medal, and I discovered a Japanese pistol."

"Be careful, Wil. Now you have me worried."

Chapter 18

The next morning, Wil and Bopau sat near the fire drinking coffee.

"What do you think the next step should be, Bopau?"

The older man rubbed his growing beard. "I've always thought that what we're looking for is in the Admiralty Islands, specifically near Manus Island. It is very volcanic, and there are fifty-thousand people on the island. Manus is heavily forested. I just have a feeling."

"Okay, then let's head back to Wewak, rent ourselves a boat, and find what we're looking for."

Bopau peered at Wil. "Why have you not told anyone what we're actually looking for?"

Wil sipped his coffee. "There are just so many things that don't make sense here, and my gut reaction is that Hank Lawrence is involved somehow as is Holloman."

"Good thought. I've never met the man you call Holloman. Is he a tall, grumpy man with a short beard?"

Wil laughed. "That would fit him to a tee. He's here?"

"I think I saw him."

"That would make sense because I believe Mr. Loe either unknowingly hired a friend of his in Stamp or is part of all of this."

"What are you going to do?"

"We're going to find what we're looking for."

Throughout the day the group made its way back to Wewak by vehicle. Later that night, the minute they arrived, most of the tired group dropped into their hotel rooms. Wil stood outside staring at the Pacific Ocean.

"Is everything okay?" Carly said, standing next to him.

"Nope, there is just something wrong about this whole mission."

She took a deep breath. "You're right. There are a lot of things happening here that none of us know about. I'm good friends with Kelsey's best friend, Gemini, and her boyfriend, Dolby. We were talking one night, and they mentioned this expedition that would bring the Lawrences billions. Gemini mentioned that Kelsey's part was to draw you in, so you could be the guide they're looking for." She sighed. "What you probably didn't know is that your family is involved with it also."

"*My* family?"

"Yes, they have a part in all of this. What it is I'm not sure; however, they all expect to gain billions of dollars, so it's more than finding a few masks. What are you looking for?"

"The less you know, the better."

That night Wil called Kelsey and got through after the second ring.

"Are you okay?" she asked. "I didn't know if I

would hear from you after our last conversation."

"Yeah, about that. I've heard so many things here about you and your parents that I'm not sure what to believe. I want to trust you, but I'm just not sure I can."

Kelsey sighed on her end. "Please, Wil, I have a lot to tell you, but don't give up on me. A lot of what they're saying was true in the very beginning, but that changed the moment I set eyes on you."

"I will always love you, but maybe it's best that we go our separate ways."

"You can't mean that, Wil. Please think about it, and at least let us talk about it when you get back."

"How can I ever trust you? You used me, and it sounds like you've done this before."

"That's how it started out. Originally, I was tasked with seducing you to help my family. That's how my family works. But that changed when I met you."

"Even at the expense of others?"

"We don't see it that way. Do you think your family is any different?"

"How do you even know my family?"

"Before you accuse me of wrong behavior, check your own backyard."

Wil heard the click of the phone on the other end.

"Is everything okay?"

Wil took Carly's hand and walked to the elevator with her.

"You sure this is what you want?"

He kissed her as the elevator went to the third floor, and she responded. He slid his key into the lock, opened the door, pushed it open, and carried her into the bed.

She started to lift his shirt, but he stopped.

"I can't do this."

Carly straightened out her clothes. "You must really love her?"

"I do, darn it."

Chapter 19

Carly joined Wil and Bopau the next morning for breakfast in the hotel.

"It's so great to have an egg," Carly said.

Wil and Bopau both had a bowl of oatmeal with toast and juice.

"Were you able to procure the boat?" Wil asked.

"We have it, and I also hired a captain who knows the islands very well."

Carly dipped her toast in the egg. "I've done some reading, and the island is known for agriculture, fishing, and trade."

Bopau nodded. "What's unique about the island are the caves underneath the ocean that people have tried to explore, but they can't find an entrance."

Wil tasted his juice. "Then our goal is to find the entrance. I would suggest the Pacific Ocean side of the island because of the strong currents."

Bopau agreed. "That would make sense. How are we going to handle this?"

"We'll set up some kind of command center on that part of the island with help from the indigenous people and look for the caves. We were able to secure larger air tanks, so we can stay down longer in the water."

Wil drank his orange juice. "We'll go down in pairs and alternate the dives. Carly and I will do the first dive, then a couple of hours later, you and Dr. Richter will dive."

"What about others?" Carly asked.

"I'm not sure if anyone else would be interested or skilled enough to dive, so we'll keep them up here at the command center to monitor everything that is going on, in particular any storms that may be coming our way." Wil took Carly's hand and walked along the beach. "I'm sorry about last night."

"Don't be. I was disappointed because I wanted to spend the night with you, but I can understand. I hope I find a guy like you."

"You will."

Once everyone was in place, they boarded the motor-powered boat that would take them to the islands. An hour later they docked on the north end of the island.

Wil climbed off the boat and stared out at the vast Pacific Ocean and then surveyed the area. He kept his eyes on a group of rocks that appeared to be a cove. Bopau joined him. "We may have found it," Wil said.

Bopau turned to where his eyes were searching. "Let's give it a try."

The group spent the next couple of hours setting up camp a bit back into the forest away from the beating waves of the ocean. Wil turned to Tyler Stamp. "I'll have you handle everything on land. Keep us under surveillance at all times, and especially keep us abreast of any storms coming in."

"Will do," he said.

"Vivian, you're joining us on the boat in case of

any incidents. Bopau, Dr. Richter, and Carly will handle the dive crews. Ivory and Sage, your jobs will be to provide us as much intelligence as you can about this area, and we will provide you from what we're finding."

Once everything was set, the boat motored to the group of rocks that Wil had seen. The captain was able to find a place where he could anchor. He pointed out to Bopau that it could get dangerous with the tides.

Wil and Carly suited up and dropped into the water. They spent a couple of hours searching but found nothing. Bopau and Dr. Richter did the same thing after lunch. The divers continued for the next three days and couldn't find anything.

Several sat on the beach discussing what they had seen.

Sage asked Wil. "Do you still think it's here?"

"My gut tells me it's around those groups of rocks, but we just haven't found it yet."

Dr. Richter jumped in. "Wil, I noticed an area on the southeast side that at times seemed like there was something shining like the sun was going through a hole."

"We'll try that first thing in the morning. This time all four of us are going to go down there, and maybe with more eyes in that area, we may find something."

He turned to Bopau. "Is there a way we can get more oxygen in the tanks?"

Bopau thought for a moment. "We could slow down the breathing apparatus, so we're taking in less air. It would still be safe, or we could wait until we get larger air tanks."

"Let's slow down the oxygen. My gut tells me

tomorrow we're going to find something."

~

The next morning the group headed back toward the rocks. This time they brought the others with them in case something went wrong. The four divers went under and swam toward the rock formations.

Two hours later Wil noticed a fissure of sorts and made his way toward it. He tried to pry the sides apart, and just like that, the sides slid sideways, and he was able to slip through. He swam a bit then surfaced toward the top of the water. What he saw was an underground cave just like Bopau had thought.

He quickly went back out of the cave and toward the surface where the others had gone. They climbed back on the boat.

"Not a blasted thing," Dr. Richter said.

"Don't be so sure. I think we've found it."

"What?" Sage said, her face excited.

"I found an underground cave or more likely an underground passage."

"Where?" Dr. Richter asked.

"I found a fissure and was able to slip through it. We'll go back tomorrow and see what we can find. It'll be dark soon, so we won't have enough time today."

That night the group stayed around the fire not wanting to go to sleep, perhaps because they were excited about what could happen the next morning.

"Is it true there could be billions of dollars down there?" Carly asked.

Dr. Richter thought about it. "There could be that, but there could also be items that we never thought about."

"Like what?" Sage asked.

"Who knows? Ancient weapons, indigenous masks, you name it. It's hard even to imagine."

"We'll find out tomorrow if there is anything," Ivory said.

Carly looked at Bopau. "What are you going to do with your share?"

"I'm not sure at this point. Perhaps I'll buy a new boat and travel to America. I've always wanted to go there."

Sage grinned. "I'm going to buy a brand-new house back in Chicago with plenty of guards and two German Shepherds."

"Two?" Carly asked.

Sage laughed. "I've always wanted two dogs."

Everyone laughed. "What about you, Carly?"

"I'd probably use the money to get my masters in archaeology. I could do this for a living." She turned to Wil. "What about you?"

"I'd have enough money to fix the roof on my cabin."

"You'd have that and plenty," Dr. Richter said. "Me, I'm going to start my own archaeology business and do what Carly has suggested—continue doing this. In fact, you'll be my first employee."

"I accept," she grinned.

They all turned at Wil's voice. "I hate to be the bearer of bad news, but ownership of historical artifacts is complex. I do know the Papua New Guinea National Museum and Gallery is responsible for preserving and protecting the cultural heritage of this area."

"That's true," Dr. Richter said. "In 2020, more than one hundred cultural artifacts were returned to the national museum and gallery after being recovered from an illegal heist in the United States."

"What are we going to do?" Carly asked.

Wil sighed. "We'll worry about it after we find the treasure."

Chapter 20

Wil was the first one up the next morning. He sat on the beach and stared toward the rocks contemplating what they could find. Bopau joined him a few minutes later and sat down by him on the beach.

"You're up early," Bopau said.

"Yeah, just thinking about what could happen today, and it's not just finding a treasure. We're being watched, and something is going to happen."

Bopau eyed him. "Why do you think that?"

Wil sighed. "Just a feeling. I hope I'm wrong."

"Many times, feelings are right. Just be aware."

"I plan on it. Let's get some food and find that treasure."

An hour later the boat headed toward the rocks once more. All four donned their suits and dived into the water. Ten minutes after the dive, Wil found the fissure once more. He squeezed through, followed by Carly, Dr. Richter, and finally Bopau.

They all floated up to the top. Wil swam toward land, and the others followed. He crawled onto the beach, pulled Carly up, and helped the others.

"Let's take our gear off here and hide it behind these rocks, and let's explore and see what we can find."

They spent the next hour searching for treasures. Wil had contacted those on the boat making them aware they were in the cave.

"Maybe we should split up?" Dr. Richter suggested.

Wil nodded. "Bopau, you and Dr. Richter go down the north passage, and we'll take the south passage. We'll meet back here in two hours."

"We'll see you then," Dr. Richter said.

Wil and Carly made their way down the tunnel for about thirty minutes when Wil came to a sudden stop. "It can't be this easy."

"What do you mean?"

Then she saw it. "That looks like a treasure chest."

The two hurried over to it. Sitting on the ground in front of them was a sealed be-jeweled wooden box. Wil slid down on his knees and slowly opened it.

"Come on, open it!" Carly said, anxiously.

"Slow down, I don't want something to jump out at me."

"Sorry. I'm just excited."

Wil slowly opened the chest. Both were stunned at what they saw. The box was filled with gold, silver, and gems.

"Oh my gosh, we've hit it," Carly said. "Is this Yamashita's gold?"

Wil shook his head. "I don't think so. That was hidden in the Philippines, but this could be one of the treasures looted during World War II."

Carly scooped her hands into it and dropped the treasure back in. Wil touched her hand. "Let's carry this back out and figure a way to get it to the boat."

They lifted it and started walking back the way they came. Carly struggled from the weight of it, but they made it back.

Wil contacted the boat. "We've found a treasure chest, but it's awfully heavy and will need some rope to pull it up."

Tyler spoke, "I can hook a rope to the boat, and we can pull it in that way."

"Let's give that a try. I'll swim out and grab the rope." He looked at Carly. "Will you be okay?"

"Yeah. I'll try to figure out a way to seal it, so it doesn't lose its contents in the ocean."

"Okay. I'll be back."

~

As soon as he dived in, Bopau and Dr. Richter walked over. "Nothing," Dr. Richter said.

They both stopped when they saw the chest. "Wow, we've found something," Dr. Richter said.

He and Bopau dug their hands into gold and gems. "This is amazing," Bopau said. "I've been looking for this for many years, but it's just a start."

"You mean there is more?" Carly asked.

"Oh yes," Bopau said. "Much more. It has to be somewhere near here."

They turned as Wil popped back out of the water. He jumped up and wrapped the rope several times around the chest. "We're following this all the way to the boat."

He pulled on the rope, and it started moving. The others jumped in after him, and they followed the chest until they reached the fissure. Wil pulled it back as the others pushed the treasure through, and they followed.

Once the chest was at the boat, they climbed out of

the water and onto the stern. They all gathered around the chest and peered at it. Everyone had no words.

Finally, Wil broke the silence. "Let's unload it into separate trays and bury it underneath the hull of the boat for the time being until we contact the museum curator."

Everyone looked at him as if he'd lost his mind.

"What?" he asked. "We can't just steal this. And we need to bargain with the Papua New Guinea government because if there is more down there, we want the other stuff."

"It makes sense," Dr. Richter said.

It took them a good portion of the afternoon to catalog the treasure. Once finished, they headed back to their campsite and barbecued hot dogs and hamburgers.

"Where did you find these?" Sage asked.

Wil grinned. "Bopau knew someone on the other side of the island who likes American food. He also brought us some beer, and we deserve it."

"I agree," Dr. Richter said.

After they finished eating, they sat around the fire talking about the treasure.

"Are you ready for a history lesson?" Sage asked.

They nodded. She grinned while sipping her beer. "During World War II, the Imperial Japanese Army looted the conquered Asian countries of their national treasures, including what we found—gold, silver, precious stones and gems, golden statues, and much more."

She opened another beer. "Probably the most famous treasure is Yamashita's gold, also known as the Yamashita treasure, which was loot stolen in Southeast Asia by Japanese forces and supposedly hidden in caves, tunnels, and underground complexes in different cities in the Philippines."

Dr. Richter jumped in. "The treasure was named after Japanese general, Tomoyuki Yamashita, who conquered Malaysia in seventy days. The problem is that the loot has lured treasure hunters from around the world for more than fifty years, and nothing has been found. Experts have dismissed its existence as mere myth."

Ivory spoke up. "Are you saying this isn't it?"

Sage shook her head. "There are other treasures out there including three sacred ones — the sword Kusanagi no Tsurugi, the mirror Yata no Kagami, and the jewel Yasakani no Magatama. Those would be magnificent finds if it's true."

Vivian turned to Dr. Richter. "Do you believe it's true?"

He thought for a moment while sipping on his beer. "I don't have any reason not to believe it."

Wil stood up. "We'll find out tomorrow what's out there, and my guess is there will be much more than what we've found."

Chapter 21

The group headed back toward the cave first thing the next morning. "We'll go down with three this time," Wil said. "Bopau, contact the museum and see what can be done with the treasure."

"Yes, Boss."

Wil took Bopau to the side away from everyone. "Contact Mr. Loe and let him know what's going on and express our concerns about all of this."

"I can do that. Be careful."

Wil joined the others, and they dived back into the water and swam toward the cave. Wil opened the fissure once more, and they went through. They climbed out of the water, took off their gear, and headed down into the cave.

"This is where we found the treasure," Wil said. "Let's go further in."

The trio traveled another hour before they came to three different tunnels. "Which way, Wil?" Carly asked.

He looked at Dr. Richter. "Any ideas?"

"None."

Wil took a deep breath. "Let's try the middle one."

They slowly walked through the tunnel which was darker than the others. Thirty minutes later they saw a light. Hurrying toward it, they stopped when they saw a Japanese soldier with a samurai sword staring at them. Before they could react, he bolted toward them.

As they backed up, Wil spoke to him in Japanese. "Slow down, big guy. We're here as friends."

The Japanese soldier responded, retaking his previous stance.

The other two stared wide-eyed at Wil. "What did he say?" Dr. Richter said.

"He's been protecting this cave for the last twenty years, and no one is to enter."

"Ask him what he's protecting?"

Wil relayed the question. The Japanese soldier spoke then glared at Richter.

"He won't tell us."

A different voice spoke in the cave. "Well maybe *he*'ll tell us."

They all turned when a shot went off that knocked the Japanese soldier down, hitting him in the shoulder.

Holloman stood there with a smirk on his face, He shoved Vivian over toward them. "We brought someone here to help with all the blood that will be spilled."

Vivian dove down and started working on the big guy's shoulder. "It's not too bad. He'll live."

"That's good," Holloman said. "Now we can find what we're looking for. Alman, did you find anything?"

"Just the treasure. And that will have to be enough because the authorities are on their way."

"Damn it, Bolton. How long, Alman?"

"They could be here right now. We have to get out of here."

Holloman turned as a couple of others walked in.

"Little brother, it's so wonderful to see you again. Thank you for what you've been able to accomplish."

Wil laughed. "I should have known you were involved in another get-rich-quick scheme."

Carly smiled and hurried over to Cole and kissed him on the cheek. "Your brother is nothing like you are."

Alman broke in. "Holloman, we must get out of here."

Holloman turned to the others. "Get rid of their gear, and let's head back to the boat. We have some sailing to do."

An evil grin enveloped Holloman's face. "It's a good thing we left the nurse with you. The only reason you're still alive is because Kelsey Lawrence asked that I spare your life. And you know I'd do anything for my daughter."

Vivian touched Wil's shoulder. "The Japanese soldier is still alive and will make it. We have to find a way to get out of here. Holloman and his group have seized control of the boat."

~

Kelsey was eating breakfast in the hotel lobby when her father came waltzing in with a big smile on his face.

"What are you so happy about?"

"They got the treasure and evaded the authorities."

"And Wil?"

"They let him live as you asked. For how long, who knows?"

"What do you mean?"

"Holloman said they didn't kill him but left him in the underwater passage without the scuba gear."

Kelsey bolted to her feet. "You said no harm would come to him."

"All I said was I wouldn't kill him outright, but it'll be up to him to find a way to survive."

"I should have known better than to trust you."

"Why would you even care what happens to the guy? Are you in love with him?"

Kelsey didn't answer.

Her father grinned. "Do you really think Wil Bolton would care about you after what you've done to him?"

Kelsey glared at him. "I just don't like the way you've manipulated people. Not everyone has to die for you to get what you want. I was better off in South Dakota with Wil."

~

Wil and Vivian struggled to carry the Japanese soldier toward a tunnel. Wil finally stopped. "I've got to find a way out of here. See what you can do for the guy."

He disappeared into the tunnel searching for a way out. Wil had travelled thirty minutes when he thought he saw some light. He scrambled toward it and found an exit to the tunnel out into a grassy, forest area. He hurried back to Vivian and the Japanese soldier. "I've found a way out."

They turned when the Japanese soldier started speaking.

Wil tried to understand. "What I can get out of it, he wants us to grab something." Wil hurried to where he pointed, then found a large sack full of items. He lifted it over his shoulder and ran back. Just then the earth started to shake. The Japanese man spoke once more.

"A volcano," Wil said. He grabbed the bag and swung it over his shoulder. Wil and Vivian struggled to transport the Japanese soldier out of the cave. They made it to the entrance just as the volcano shot up into the air several hundred yards behind them. Rocks flew into the Pacific Ocean, and lava poured down the other side.

"Somebody up above is watching over us," Vivian said.

They began the slow walk down the path stopping every few moments to catch their breath. An hour later they froze when small men pointed spears at them. They started speaking in their native tongue which Wil did not understand.

The Japanese talked back to them and turned to Wil and spoke in his language. "They want to know if we need help."

"You bet we do," Wil said.

Chapter 22

Nolan took a sip of his martini. "Your dad sure does put on some wild parties."

"I'm used to it," Kelsey said. "I've been coming to these since I was thirteen. It got old after a while."

"Here you are doing it once more. Did you miss it when you were with Bolton?"

She peered at him. "I'm not going to talk about Wil ever with you."

"Do you love him?"

"I told you I'm not speaking to you about Wil. Now if you'll excuse me, I'm going to grab a drink." As she waited at the bar, Kelsey turned when Mr. Loe stood beside her. "Mr. Loe, what are you doing here?"

He grinned. "Your father wanted to rub it in my face that he found this large treasure in Papua New Guinea."

"That would be my father. Did you hear if everyone is okay?"

"I haven't heard. Your father is out there, or is he really your father?"

"Holloman? He's not my father, but I know he used it to get close to Wil."

Mr. Loe peered into her eyes. "You realize that it's

going around that you had a big part in the seduction of Wil Bolton and this whole operation."

She took a deep breath. "I did, and I'm disappointed in myself. I went in with the idea of seducing Wil, but I never thought I'd fall in love with him, but I am in love with him. He'll never want to talk to me or see me after what's happened."

"It would be tough," he agreed. "From what I've seen though, Wil is a peculiar kind of man, so who knows what will happen? The one thing I will say is you need to come clean with him if you want to have a lasting relationship."

"I've tried, but after this I don't know if it will ever happen again." She eyed him. "This time I have a question for you. Why are you so nice to me after what I've done?"

"You did what you were told to do. Let me ask you a question: if you would have known Wil before you were assigned this task, would you have gone through with it?"

"No way. I'd seriously thought about staying right there in that broken-down cabin with Wil, and to this day I wish I had. I would have been happy waiting for him when he went on his adventures. We planned everything together in that cabin, and I've never done that with any guy. I even told him about my other affairs, and he didn't flinch or judge me."

Mr. Loe sipped on his drink. "That tells me right there Wil's the guy for you. Don't let him go."

"It's too late."

"It never is. In most people's eyes, I should have dumped my wife for what she did. I couldn't because she's the gal I want to spend my life with. She makes me feel whole, so we had a long conversation as two grown adults about what had happened, not one dominating over the other. You and Wil are like that, and if you just let him talk to you, you'll be fine. True love is so hard to find. Don't let it go now that you have it."

Chapter 23

The village traditional healer did all he could to help Tito, the Japanese soldier. Wil had found out his name in one of his rare quiet moments. Now Wil sat down on the beach and stared at the waves hitting the beach. How he wished Lydia was still alive.

If Lydia was alive, where would their relationship go after the last few months? He would have to tell her about Kelsey, and that would end it for the two of them, and he'd be back where he started.

He stood up and stared at the ocean one more time. Who was he fooling? Lydia was not alive, and even if she was, the girl in his heart was Kelsey. He climbed up and walked back to the village. Vivian sat near the fire with a couple of the villagers, who sipped on drinks.

She noticed him and asked him to join her. "This drink is very good."

"What is it?" Wil asked.

"*Paiya wara.* It's good, old-fashioned moonshine."

Wil took a drink, and his face soured. "Wow, that is firewater."

Vivian laughed. "Apparently it is made from the leftovers from fruit, of which there a lot in Papua New Guinea."

Wil grinned and sat down. "No wonder they have so many exotic dances." He'd sat on the beach every night for the past two weeks waiting for Bopau and a boat to show up to take them back to America.

Just then a boat came in his way. As it moved closer, he saw Bopau waving vigorously. The boat pulled up to a dock, and Bopau jumped off and ran toward Wil.

The little guy gave him a hug. "I'm so happy you're okay. And the others?"

"Tito is wounded, but Vivian is okay. The others were part of the group who took the treasure."

Bopau frowned. "They made it out of the country with it."

"Doesn't surprise me. What about the other items?"

"They know nothing and don't care. I know nothing about any other items."

Wil grinned. "We struck it rich, partner."

"Partner?"

"Yep, if you want, you're going with me on every new adventure."

"I go, but Mr. Loe sure needs to do a better job of finding trustworthy people."

"You got that right. We'll have to tell him that when we return to America. Now that Tito's better, we can go back."

"That is the Japanese soldier's name?"

Wil nodded. "I finally pried it out of him."

The two hurried back to the village, and Wil saw that Tito sat up with Vivian attending to him. She had been sitting with the villagers but must have moved over to Tito while Wil was gone. He had a sour look when she gave him a drink. He spit it out and said something. Wil laughed.

Bopau looked at him. "What did he say?"

"Tastes like horse manure."

The next morning, they loaded the boat and sailed toward Wewak where the plane waited for them. There would be fewer passengers going back than there was on the initial trip. but this time there would be some important Japanese artifacts heading to America.

Wil stood on the deck and stared out into the water. Vivian stood next to him. "This was an interesting trip," she said. "I can't wait until the next one."

"Yes, it had its ups and downs, but overall, it turned out pretty well. Hopefully, next time will be a little bit smoother."

"It will," Vivian said. "You'll be there with us."

~

The group landed in San Diego two days later. They would spend the night there before flying back to Chicago.

Wil spent the afternoon and night walking along the beach. He had a lot on his mind and didn't know how to handle some of it. Truth was he cared a lot about Kelsey. As much as he thought Kelsey was beautiful, Wil knew they could never be together because they were from two different worlds. Sooner or later, she would get tired of his world and want to go back to her own, plus there was all the garbage that had taken place with Treasure Paradise. He couldn't be sure if she truly cared about him, but he did know that he loved her. He just didn't know if he could live with her.

After dark, Wil sat on the beach and stared out at the ships floating by. It was such a cool sight. He turned to voices in the distance. A couple was walking hand-in-hand along the beach, and every once in a while, the man would reach over and kiss her.

Wil had heard that San Diego was a romantic town. He pushed off the sand and headed to his hotel room for a good night's sleep.

The next day the plane was in the air heading to Chicago where Mr. Loe waited for them and their treasures. The two had talked over the past couple of days about what had happened, and Mr. Loe said he was pretty disappointed in the group he had put together.

It was midafternoon when the plane landed in Chicago. Mr. Loe and his wife, along with a couple of security guards, were waiting for them at baggage claim. That night there would be a banquet to display what the group had found, followed by a gallery exhibition the next night.

As soon as he checked into the hotel, Wil put on a suit and headed to the Loe's mansion.

Already there were Bopau, Vivian, and Tito. Wil smiled. "Bopau, you and Tito clean up nice."

"What about me?" Vivian asked.

Wil grinned. "You're also nifty."

She laughed. "I'm glad you didn't say gorgeous because we both know that's a lie. The gal over there is gorgeous." Vivian took Tito's hand, and the two walked away.

Bopau grinned. "Those two seemed to have hit it off. Did you know the guy speaks English well?"

"How can that be after living in the cave for so many years?"

Bopau laughed. "He made us think that, but he

spent three years in America before he ended up back in Japan and in the war. He told Vivian and me that he guarded the treasures with his father until he passed on four years ago. Then it was his sole job to guard the cave. Once we came, that was over. He is considered a war criminal, but that's our secret."

Holloman joined them. "Well, Wil Bolton, you made it out of that dingy cave. I'm happy for you but happier that we came back with all those millions in jewels."

"Did you throw my brother, Cole, down one of your holes?"

He laughed. "Nope, he can be useful in the future. What is this big find that you brought tonight?"

"I haven't even looked in the bag. For all I know it could be a mask or a pygmy head. It's all Mr. Loe's."

Holloman laughed. "Where are you heading next?"

"I don't know, but I'm sure we'll see each other along the way."

"Count on it. We're actually competitors, and it's interesting to see who will come out on top."

"Someday you'll do something on your own."

They turned as Mr. Loe came to the podium. Wil slipped back out of the way as Mr. Loe started speaking. Kelsey was looking his way. She spun away when their eyes met. He turned back to listen to Mr. Loe talk about his acquisitions.

"There were several interesting items, thanks to our friend, Tito. He spent the last fifteen years of his life guarding this sacred treasure."

They clapped and Tito bowed.

Mr. Loe pulled the first two items out of the bag. "First, we have a couple of skull hooks. These are sacred objects of the Kerewa people. These flat board-like figures were created for the display of human skulls. In the past, headhunting was important in religious practices throughout the region because it honored the spirits whose power sustained the community."

Mr. Loe's eyes scanned the room. "Next, we have a mask. It's a mask from the mid-19th century called a Murik mask from the Murik Lagoon of the coastal Sepik River. Its size measures just under twenty-three inches. The estimated cost ranges from sixty thousand to eighty thousand dollars, but it isn't for sale. It'll be displayed in our gallery as will all of these artifacts."

Everyone gasped at the last item pulled out of the bag. "A Japanese samurai sword, and it's magnificent—something I've always wanted to find and finally have. The *katana* is a Japanese sword characterized by a curved, single-edged blade with a circular or squared guard and long grip to accommodate two hands. Samurai warriors used the sword in feudal Japan."

Everyone clapped once Mr. Loe was finished showing the artifacts.

"This is perfectly amazing, and I would like to thank all of those who had a hand in finding these artifacts. Tomorrow night, we'll be placing them in our gallery with a special celebration, so please join us. Enjoy yourself."

Chapter 24

Wil texted Kelsey and asked her to meet him at the pier on Lake Michigan. She arrived at four-thirty and saw Wil staring out onto the lake.

She joined him. "Are you okay?"

"Not really. I had hoped to become a treasure hunter but didn't expect anything like this. I knew your family was involved, but now my brother, Cole, was in the underground passage and my guess is you knew about it."

"I did."

He turned to her. "And you never said one damn word to me."

"What was I supposed to say? Your family is as crooked as mine. I had hoped to spare you any pain, but all I've done is caused heartache all the way around." Neither said anything. Finally, Kelsey spoke up. "Why are we here?"

He took a deep breath. "I can't do this anymore. You and I can't be together. I can't trust you, and trust is a critical issue in my life."

"You really don't understand how our family operates. There is a code that the Lawrence family lives by. To screw as many people as they can and become rich in the process. I'm no different. I spent all night making love with you because I wanted to glean information from you, but you're so damn quiet."

"So, any of the nights we were together meant nothing to you?"

She peered into his eyes. "They meant everything to me, and not because I wanted information from you, but because I gave you my heart, and I can never take it back. No matter what happens from this moment forward, you'll always have it." Kelsey took a deep breath. "We'll never be together again. No matter what you think, you love me, and we both know it. This is a crappy situation all the way around, and if I had it to do over there is no way I would have left your cabin. Now it's too late because you'll never forgive me for what I've done."

"I thought you said you were scared about me not being around."

"I thought I would be, but I wasn't. I was worried about you all the time, but I always hoped you'd walk back through that cabin door. I'd be there waiting for you, and everything would be the same as it had always been. You don't realize how much I'm in love with you."

"Are you? A person who loves someone doesn't do what you did to me."

"You hypocrite. How did it feel spending time with Carly, or was it Sage? Or was it both? Why would you do that to me?"

"Nothing happened."

"Yeah, right. I can't trust you either. We should go our separate ways. I thought we could start all over and make it work."

"It won't happen. I'm out of here. Go back to Nolan or whatever boy toy you have this week."

She glared at him. "You're acting like a jerk. Wil, you were never a boy toy."

~

Holloman sipped his wine as he gazed at the pool. "Any clue where we're traveling to next, Boss?"

"I have no clue at this point. Loe is really closed mouth when he talks about upcoming trips. He doesn't trust anyone other than Wil Bolton."

"Are you worried about him and Kelsey?"

"No, Kelsey has Bolton wrapped around her finger. I'm not concerned."

They both looked up as Kelsey strutted into the pool area.

"Wow, don't you look nice."

"Where are you off to tonight?" her father asked.

"I decided to join some friends out on the town."

"Is Nolan joining you?"

"I haven't talked to him today. Besides, isn't he out of town?"

"He is. I forgot about that," her father said.

"Yeah, right," she said. "I'll see you tomorrow."

"Any word on where Bolton is heading next?"

"I told you I'm not doing it anymore."

Holloman frowned at her. "Why do you even care about Bolton?"

Kelsey shook her head. "Holloman, you really have no clue who Wil Bolton is, do you?"

Her father pointed at a seat. "Why don't you sit down and tell us?"

She grinned. "And lose my advantage over the two of you? Forget it."

Later that night Kelsey joined her friends at one of the nightclubs downtown. On a Friday night it was usually pretty crowded, and tonight wasn't any different. She surveyed the room to see if there were any others she knew. Kelsey stopped when her eyes spotted Wil sitting with a Japanese guy and someone from the Pacific Island area. She couldn't believe he would be here. A couple of ladies strutted over to them. One gal introduced the other two to the guy from the South Pacific. The other gal sat next to the Japanese man.

"Isn't that Wil Bolton?" Alexis asked, coming back with some drinks. Alexis and Kelsey had been good friends for many years.

Kelsey looked toward where she nodded. "It sure looks like him."

"Should we invite him over?"

"No, it looks like he is with others."

"The more the merrier," JJ, Alexis's boyfriend, said. "I'll go ask them."

Kelsey took a deep breath as JJ approached the group. He came back, looking sheepish.

"What happened?" Alexis said.

"The one guy speaks Japanese and the other spoke some other language, but Bolton could translate both and they both said no."

The others laughed. The music started playing again, and everyone but Kelsey went out onto the dance floor. Kelsey looked over and only Wil sat there. She chuckled as the two foreigners were trying to dance with the gals.

"You should have seen Bopau dancing in the Pacific Islands to the native drums. He did surprisingly well."

Kelsey peered into Wil's eyes. "I'm sure that was pretty cool. What are you doing here, especially after you told me we were through?"

"Didn't you say the same thing? They invited me to go out with them before I head back to South Dakota."

She grinned. "You know I frequent this place, and you wanted to see me one more time."

Wil laughed. "You figured me out."

She took a deep breath. "I wouldn't mind if you spend the night with me before you fly back to South Dakota."

"What about Nolan?"

"He's out of town for the evening."

She turned to where Wil was pointing. "Maybe somebody should tell him that."

Kelsey turned around to say something to Wil, but he was gone. She felt an arm snake around her waist and peered up at Nolan. "I thought you were out of town."

"Just got back a little bit ago. I hear Bolton is on his way to New York City to check out some new group who's interested in joining his treasure hunt. Oh, tell your father the group is called Archaeological Synopsis, or something like that."

"Interesting, but he didn't say anything to me about it, but then again he probably wouldn't."

"What happened?"

Kelsey sighed. "Our best contact told me to buzz off."

Chapter 25

It had been three weeks since Wil and Kelsey had their disagreement on the pier. Kelsey had tried to call him several times, but he wouldn't answer. She drove down to her attorney's office to sign paperwork selling the company to her employees. They deserved having an employee-owned business where they could make the money she'd been making over the past seven years.

The attorney came out to bring her into his office. "Are you sure this is what you want, Kelsey?"

"Positive. Everything I want sits in a cabin in South Dakota."

"Okay, let's get this done."

Over the next thirty minutes, Kelsey signed several documents, and the attorney provided her with a check for five-million dollars. "You realize this isn't even close to what the business is worth."

"I know, but they have to have somewhere to start, and I don't want to take everything from them."

"This is not you, Kelsey."

She smiled. "What can I do? I'm a gal who is in love with some guy from South Dakota."

"I wish you the best of luck."

"Thanks for everything you've done for me."

"It was a pleasure."

Kelsey arrived in Rapid City later that afternoon. She grabbed her gear and the keys for a rental car but took a seat. What if he rejected her? All she knew was she wasn't leaving Wil ever again. He would have to physically throw her out. As she started down the road, her cell phone rang. She put it on the speaker phone.

Her father was yelling. "What are you doing selling your business? Where are you?"

"It's none of your business. I'm through with the Lawrence family drama."

"You're in South Dakota with the guy you manipulated to get what you wanted."

"No, to get what *you* wanted. And again, it's none of your business where I am or what I'm doing. I'm through with your family."

"You realize you're making a big mistake. Now Bolton will die."

"He won't. Remember, if anyone harms him in any way, I will make sure everyone knows exactly what the Lawrence family is doing."

Her father laughed. "You'll always be a Lawrence."

"I won't, but I will protect Wil any way I can. Remember that. We're through." She disconnected and smiled to herself. It felt good.

Kelsey pulled into Wil's driveway and saw him sitting on the porch. "Do you ever sit anywhere else?"

"What do you want? I thought I made it clear I don't want anything to do with you."

She climbed out of the car, ambled over to him, and sat down. "We're not through by any means. I'm here to stay with you for the rest of our lives."

He stood up. "Not likely."

For the next eight days, the two had minimal conversations. A good morning here, a good night there. Kelsey did everything she could to start a conversation.

One night Wil sat out on the porch and Kelsey joined him.

"I really love sitting out here at night, but especially in the morning. It does help that you're here also."

Wil just turned and glared at her.

She grinned. "You can glare at me all you want, but the truth is—we belong together, and you know it. I'll never leave you; nor will I ever do anything to hurt you."

"Right."

"What is that supposed to mean?"

"First, you dress all sexy-like on Deadwood's Main Street, knowing exactly what you're doing, then you tell me you're in love with me. Then you show up with your fiancé, Nolan, and tell me all about how you used me."

"Yeah, I'm sorry about all that."

"Don't be sorry. Just go away."

Kelsey glared at him. "Get it through your thick skull I'm not going away ever."

Wil stood up and lifted her over his shoulder.

"What are you doing?"

He carried her into the room and gently set her down on the bed.

"Don't you dare touch one piece of my clothing unless you truly love me."

He just stared at her then turned on his heel.

"Wil, please stop."

He turned to her. "Will you ever forgive me?"

He took a deep breath. "I already have forgiven you."

Kelsey walked into the bedroom Wil slept in, slid in next to him, and wrapped her arms around him. "If you've forgiven me, why do you keep bringing up the past?"

Wil was silent.

"Please, answer my question."

He squeezed her hands gently. "It hurts so bad. I finally found a woman whom I genuinely loved with all my heart and found out she was just using me for her own gain. You own a multi-million-dollar business, your dad is a billionaire, your mother tells me you get two million dollars a year from your father as an allowance, and then you manipulate me and others for millions of dollars from a treasure hunt. How much money is enough?"

She kissed him on the forehead. "That about sums up my life. However, my life changed when I first set eyes on you in Deadwood. I wanted to be a different person because I want to be in your life, but it took me a while because I'm still a Lawrence, and it's not that easy to break away from something I've been brought up in." She kissed him once more. "You make me feel so different than anyone ever has. When I hold your hands, I feel the tingle that shoots to my heart, and when you put your arms around me, I feel safe for the first time in my life. When we make love, it's out of this world. I've told you many times my heart belongs to you, and it always will." She squeezed him tightly. "Get some sleep because I'm not leaving you tonight."

Chapter 26

Wil was sitting out on the porch when Kelsey came out to join him in one of his t-shirts. He looked up at her. "You know it is winter."

She grinned. "You do care about me."

"No, Kelsey, I just don't want you to freeze to death in this cabin. Think of all the paperwork I'd have to deal with."

She laughed and sat down next to him. "It's been a month, and you haven't had one call to do anything spectacular in the Black Hills. It's telling you something."

"If you're thinking I'm going back to Treasure Paradise, you're nuts."

"You are, Wil, and the only reason you're not doing it is because you think I have something to do with it. I don't. I've washed my hands of all of it, and Mr. Loe is the one running it."

They both turned as a car pulled up. Maddie jumped out of the car and ran over to Wil. "We haven't heard from you in a month. What is wrong with you?"

Tessa walked over with Jonathan. "Maddie, enough."

Wil stood up and took the two kids' hands.

"You're right, I haven't been a good uncle. We'll leave these two alone."

Kelsey sighed. "I've messed him up big time, and I'm so sorry for that."

Tessa sat down next to her and put her arm around her. "It's amazing you're still here or even more amazing he hasn't sent you packing. That's a good thing."

"How is that a good thing? He rarely says anything to me, and if he does it's something derogatory about my family or me. I've tried everything I can think of to work with him. Nothing is working. If he wants me, he's going to have to come to me, but if he does, I'll never let him go again."

Tessa took a deep breath. "I need to have a talk with my little brother."

Kelsey's eyes widened. "Don't you dare. I made this mess, and I'll find a way out of it. We had our first candid conversation last night, so there is hope. I hurt him tremendously. It took him long enough to tell me that."

Tessa rolled her eyes. "That's Wil. He has a tough time expressing himself, but for some reason he's not giving up on you."

"I told myself I'm not going anywhere. Wil's the guy I'm going to be with for the rest of my life. He just doesn't know it yet."

Tessa laughed. "He knows because if he didn't feel the same way, you'd be gone pronto."

She stood. "No matter what you believe, I do need to talk to him because he's impacting my kids, and when it hurts Maddie and Jonathan, it becomes my thing."

Kelsey touched Tessa's hands. "Forgive me. I didn't mean for that to happen. I'll pack up and leave right away."

"Don't you dare leave him. He needs you just like you need him. Wil's just being his stubborn self. I'll talk to him."

Wil and the kids came out. Tessa eyed her little brother. "Wil, we need to talk."

Maddie grinned. "Uncle Wil, you're in trouble now. I told you to straighten yourself out."

Wil grinned and tousled her hair. "You're always right."

~

Wil and Tessa were walking toward the creek after she asked to talk to him in private. "I don't want to hear it, Tessa. It's none of your business what is happening with Kelsey and me."

"I'm not here to stick up for you or her. I'm here because my two children miss their uncle, and they're having a tough time understanding why you're acting like you are. They think they did something wrong, and that's why you don't see them."

"We both know that's not true. They would never do anything to hurt me; nor would I do anything to hurt them."

"They still miss you terribly and want you in their lives. When are you going to move past this pettiness with Kelsey?"

"Pettiness? She destroyed many people's lives, and you're just telling me to forget about it?"

"Why is she even here if you feel that way?"

Wil stopped and stared at his older sister. "I do love her, but what happened between the two of us hurt me so bad—all of it. I need to be able to trust her, and I don't know if I can."

"I know it hurts, but don't you think she feels the same way? Can she trust you? But if you don't believe she's trustworthy, you're crazy. She called me one time and told me exactly what happened between the two of you. I never said anything because you're a big boy and should be able to work through your own issues."

Wil sighed and peered at the wide-open area. "I wouldn't know that."

"Of course, you wouldn't because you're just thinking about yourself. Believe me, Kelsey is doing everything she can to make peace with you. She loves you more than anyone else ever has. You've made mistakes in your past, and people have forgiven you. Why can't you forgive her and move forward? You two are going to have a wonderful life, and you know it."

"Yeah, we will. But damn, Tessa, I just can't get over the fact that she messed with my head."

"Of course, you can. Forgive her, marry her, have a family, and move on with your life. And for what it's worth, find those treasures and artifacts. Kelsey will be right here waiting for you."

Wil put his arm around Tessa. "That's one thing I never doubted."

Chapter 27

After Wil and Kelsey sat through a quiet supper, Kelsey stood up. "I'm going for a walk."

"Do you mind if I join you?"

She eyed him. "I don't want to be ridiculed."

"I'm through with that." He took her hand which surprised her. The two headed towards the creek.

"I'm sorry about how I've treated you."

Kelsey stopped and peered into his eyes. "Don't you dare apologize because your sister asked you to. Only do it if you mean it."

Wil grinned. "One of the things I love about you is your sassy moods. It's a sincere apology."

The two continued walking until they arrived at the creek. Wil sat on a log, and Kelsey joined him. He took her hand.

"I've always enjoyed sitting down here by the creek," Wil said. "I enjoy it even more when you're here."

Kelsey didn't say anything; she just listened to the water running through the creek.

He turned to her. "Are you on vacation or something, because I noticed you haven't done anything with your clothing and design company?"

She turned to him. "If you would have talked to me, you would have found out that I sold it."

His eyes widened. "Why would you do that?"

"Because, you goofball, you're the one who means the most to me — not a million-dollar business or my family — you. I've loved you since the first moment I met you, and I've tried so hard the last few weeks to tell you and show you, but you're so blasted stubborn you don't listen."

She turned to him. "How many times do I have to tell you that all the things I've done are to protect you. Right now, my father is sending someone to take care of you, and if that happens, it'll be my fault and there's nothing I can do about it. Nothing at all. I gave my heart to you, Wilton Edgar Bolton. It scares me to death to do something like that, but you're worth it. I just wish you would realize that I'm worth it and will be here with you through everything that comes our way." She started to jump up, but Wil grabbed her and pulled her down toward him.

"What are you doing?"

"Are you saying you really sold your business?"

Kelsey turned to him. "I've signed all the documents needed to sell the business to the employees, but I have thirty days to make a final decision. I want to keep the business because it's truly something I did on my own. However, if I had to choose between you and the business, I'd choose you first every time."

"I don't want you to sell your business," Wil said quietly.

She held his hands. "I don't want to ever lose you."

He kissed her, and she responded passionately.

~

Wil's eyes popped open, sensing eyes were on him. Kelsey smiled at him. "Last night was wonderful, but that's the problem with us."

"What do you mean?" Wil sat up and leaned against the headboard.

She leaned against his shoulder. "What I mean is it's wonderful when we make love, but the rest of our life is so discombobulated right now, and I don't want that. I'm sure you don't want that either." Kelsey took a deep breath. "I came out here to try to mend our relationship because you're the guy I genuinely love and want to spend my life with. However, I've been here almost two weeks, and rarely have you even talked to me, then you give me a half-hearted apology, and like a dummy, I climb into bed with you."

She turned Wil's head toward her. "It doesn't work that way. You gave me an apology because your sister asked you to. In some way you meant it, but you're still upset with me. I've tried everything I can to make this work, but I can't do this anymore. So I'm flying back to Chicago today. If you want me, I mean really want to make our relationship work, it's up to you."

Kelsey started to get out of bed. Wil gently grabbed her arm and she turned to him. "I do love you and want to be with you, but everything is just so hard right now."

She reached over and kissed him. "That's one thing I've always known—that you love me just like I love you."

Chapter 28

Wil climbed into his pickup and drove down Nemo Road toward Rapid City to talk to an investment broker to help him with his money. He still couldn't believe he'd received a two-million-dollar check; nor could he even imagine that much money in a lifetime.

After about an hour with the investment broker, they had the funds set up. Wil had made sure there was money set aside for the kids' college fund—five thousand dollars a year for the next ten years. He knew it wouldn't cover the cost of school, but it would be a start.

He also invested in some money-market funds, and he signed up for a checking account that would gain at least five-percent interest each month. He placed half a million dollars into that for his personal needs. With the rest, the investor would buy stock, and let Wil know about every investment he bought or sold.

"This looks good," the broker said. "Here's what should happen after five years. Your market fund should more than double, and the kids' college fund could also double depending on the market. You've made some wise investments."

As Wil left the brokerage firm, he looked down at

his cell phone. Tessa wanted him to join her and the kids for dinner. More than an hour later, Wil knocked on the door, and Maddie answered.

"There's the cutest girl in the world," he said, lifting her up. He turned to Tessa. "How are you doing?" Wil asked.

"Work is hectic, but the kids are helping around the house. We have a treat for you tonight. I bought a grill, and Jonathan wants you to help him grill hamburgers."

"I can do that."

"He's been looking forward to it."

Wil and Jonathan went to the backyard and started the grill. Maddie joined them.

Thirty minutes later the burgers were ready. The family sat around the table enjoying hamburgers, potato salad, pork and beans, and lemonade.

"You did a good job, Jonathan," Wil said. "These taste very good."

Jonathan beamed. "I want to learn to cook. Can you help me?"

"Of course, I will. Next time it'll be steak. Your mother loves a good t-bone."

"I don't like steaks," Maddie said.

Tessa eyed her daughter. "You've never had a steak, dear, so you don't know if you like it or not."

After supper, the four played a couple of board games, then Tessa tucked them in bed. She came back out and sat with Wil. "Are you sure you're okay?"

Wil sighed. "I'm still upset about our family—how in the world did they get involved in the treasure hunt?"

"It doesn't surprise me that they were involved. Our grandparents always wanted more money, and we both know how lazy our other brothers are, so if it's easy money, they're right in."

Tessa peered at Wil. "Are you really unemployed?"

"I am," he said, sipping his lemonade. "What I'm going to do, I have no clue right now. I did read a couple of magazines on start-up businesses, so maybe that would be something."

"Good idea. The bank does offer start-up loans for businesses if you're interested. That could be helpful."

"By the way, I started a college fund for Maddie and Jonathan today."

"You didn't have to do that, but thank you." Tessa laughed. "At times Maddie believes she's already in college."

Wil sipped his drink. "Everything about this whole Treasure Paradise is fishy. I found out last week that the Lawrences and Loes split profits fifty-fifty, no matter what they find."

"That sounds weird, especially if the two are competing," Tessa said.

"Like I said, it's all weird, and I'm glad I'm out of it."

"What are your feelings for Kelsey?"

"I can't trust her."

"Trust has always been important to you. What about cute Carly?"

Wil laughed. "Are you trying to hook me up with someone?"

She frowned. "I just hate to see you lonely."

"Ideally, I wish I could go back to the time before Lydia died in that car wreck. Life was so simple."

Chapter 29

The next morning Wil was at the hardware store looking for paint for the walls in the cabin. He had been thinking about blue, but the gal who handled the paint colors suggested a more subtle shade such as breezeway or tranquil gray or even beige. He chose breezeway and left.

When his phone vibrated, he pulled over to the side of the road and picked it up.

"Wil, how are you doing?"

"Mr. Hampton, I'm doing well. What can I do for you?"

"Can you join me for lunch at twelve-thirty? I have a proposal for you."

"I'll be there."

He drove toward Custer and pulled into the parking lot in front of the cafe. When he walked in, he saw Hampton and Sheriff Kanter sitting together. He grinned and walked over. "If you two are together, this can't be good."

They both laughed. Hampton handed him a menu. "Order some food. It's on me."

"Okay, what is going on?"

"Order, then we'll talk."

They ordered their lunch, and once the server left, Hampton peered at the sheriff, who nodded. Hampton took a deep breath. "What's happened the last few months hasn't been the best days of my life. I screwed up by listening to a good friend of mine, Ben Lawrence, when I fired you. That should have never happened, and I can't take it back."

He sipped on his water. "Sheriff Kanter and I have been talking with other law-enforcement officials around the area in both South Dakota and Wyoming. The forest service doesn't have the money to hire a wildlife biologist because of budget cuts, but the sheriff's department needs people who know the Black Hills well, and you do."

Sheriff Kanter jumped in. "Wil, the sheriff's department would like to hire you as an independent contractor, meaning we would pay you when we need your services. The forest service is agreeable to doing the same thing. If we run across people who are lost, or we need help in areas we're not familiar with, we'll contact you. In addition, we and the forest service would use you when we have wild animal issues."

Hampton leaned forward. "Neither of us could provide your health benefits because you wouldn't be a full-time employee, but we would fairly compensate you either hourly or by a package. By package, I mean we would set a fee no matter how long you're out." He took a breath. "An hourly rate would be thirty dollars an hour while a package rate would be a set rate of five hundred dollars no matter how long the job would take. It would be your choice, but you would specifically work for these entities and no others."

Wil finished drinking some water. "Would it

include leading hikes or snowmobile rides—things like that?"

Hampton thought about it. "It could include that, but we never thought about it. I'm willing to work that in."

"What do I need to do?"

"You would need to sign some contracts saying you would be working with us on a contractual basis or a retainer's fee, if you prefer that term. Amanda would be your contact for any of the agencies. If the sheriff's department had an issue, they would contact Amanda, who would then call you and let you know what's happening."

"What about helicopter access?"

Sheriff Kanter answered. "The county chopper will assist when needed."

"How did this come about?" Wil asked.

Hampton sighed. "More people and animals are coming to the Black Hills, and we don't have the resources to protect both, so we need someone like you who knows every inch of the Hills. You'll be rescuing people and chasing down criminals."

"When would you like me to start?"

"Today would be great. All you have to do is sign some documents, and we're set to go," Hampton said.

"I'll think about it," Wil said.

The next afternoon Boris Loe called Wil.

"I'm surprised to hear from you," Wil said.

Boris laughed. "I'm a persistent kind of guy. Now about the Africa trip."

"I thought you would have gone by now."

"Oh no, I still have details to work out, and of course, I have to put together a team."

"Hopefully it's better than the last group."

Boris laughed once more. "I screwed that one up royally, and that's the reason for the call. I want *you* to put together the team. Several hundred applications are sitting in front of me, and since you know what it's like to be in the field, you'd be perfect to figure out who'd best handle the job."

This time Wil laughed. "Yeah, right. I couldn't figure out that Kelsey Lawrence used me, as did Sage, Carly, Dr. Richter—you name it."

"In your defense, Kelsey is particularly good at what she does, so it doesn't surprise me. In fact, a clothing and design convention will be held this weekend, and it'll give you a chance to answer some of the questions that have been nagging the both of us. In particular, drug and diamond smuggling in the shipments."

"You really believe that's happening?"

"I wouldn't put it past Hank and Ben Lawrence. Now Kelsey Lawrence is different. I don't think she'd be knowingly involved in that sort of thing, but then again, I've been wrong about a lot of things. However, before we talk about the new group, I'd like you to fly to New York City and talk to some guys about some new finds."

Wil was quiet. "Why not? I'll fly in on Saturday."

"Great, we'll talk when you arrive."

The next morning Wil sat in the Rapid City Airport waiting for his flight to Chicago. He had a couple of layovers and would be in the Windy City late afternoon. After that he would find out one last time where he and Kelsey stood.

He pulled out a piece of paper from his pocket and

chuckled as he read it. Maddie had written down all the information he'd need for a prenuptial agreement between him and Kelsey. Of course, it wouldn't hold up in any court of law, but Maddie had suggested something like this, so he and Kelsey both knew where they stood.

The plane landed in Chicago at three-thirty, and it took Wil another hour to collect his baggage and drive to the hotel he was staying in downtown on the pier. Around five-thirty he found Kelsey's condominium.

A man opened the door. "Can I help you?"

"Brandon, what are you doing here? I'm looking for Kelsey Lawrence. I must have the wrong address."

"Wil, it's good to see you."

He heard Kelsey's voice. "Who is it, Brandon?"

"Wil Bolton is looking for you."

When Kelsey saw Wil, she stopped in her tracks. "Brandon, I'll handle this." She stepped outside and took his hands. "It isn't what you think it is."

"I don't think anything. I stopped by to talk, but I see you have a date tonight."

"I do, but again, it's not what you think. I'm not into him, at least not yet. Maybe in the future. The question is what are you doing here?"

Wil sighed. "I have spent…Never mind, you enjoy your date. I'm going to my hotel and stare at Lake Michigan. You do look beautiful."

When Kelsey gripped his hands, Wil peered into her eyes, reached over, and kissed her on the lips. "I wish you all the best."

Chapter 30

Sunday morning Wil jetted toward New York City with an estimated arrival time of half past one. After this trip he would head back to Nemo and try to put his life back together. It would be hard because he was in love with Kelsey.

His mind scrambled back to what he was doing in New York City—visiting with the Archaeological Synopsis group. They were an artifact-searching group. At the present they were searching for a Viking helmet or specifically the Gjermundbu helmet. One had been found near Buskerud, Norway, but many believed there were more in America.

Wil also read a Norwegian coin had been found in Maine, as well as comb fragments, iron utensils, chess pieces, and ship fragments in other places in the country.

Needless to say, Wil was excited about the possibilities. Once he'd left LaGuardia, he found a room at a downtown hotel. He lay down on the bed and was fast asleep as soon as he hit the pillow. The next morning, he was up and ready for his meeting with the bosses at Archaeological Synopsis. They were waiting for him when he came down to the lobby.

"Mr. Bolton?"

"Yes, sir."

"I'm Colin Jurgens and this is my business partner, Arnold Drexel. Welcome to New York City and thank you for joining us for a tour of our business."

"Lead the way."

Wil hopped into their fancy Lexus, drove to downtown Manhattan, and pulled up in front of a large building with a small sign introducing their company.

Jurgens grinned. "Small signs but big hearts. We care about preserving our world's history."

"That's why Mr. Loe wanted me to talk to you."

"Come on in," Drexel said.

The three men went into the building and entered a small office that had three other employees. They headed to the back into a room where there were books laid out on a desk.

"This is what we're looking for," Drexel said. "And we've had no luck at all."

Wil gazed down at the photos and saw the helmet, then scanned what the note said. He turned to the other two. "Wasn't there a helmet found in Norway?"

"There was," Jurgens said. "However, there is believed to be another one that is near a major Viking treasure. Some have said Minnesota by the Kensington Runes; others have said Maine- and still others have said Newfoundland. We're not sure where it is, but we know it's out there. And we want you to find it."

"That will be tough because it could be anywhere."

"True," Drexel said, "but we've narrowed it down to the three places. Everyone believes it is buried underground, but there is a good chance it could be hidden in a tunnel or under a river."

"Let me take all this information back to our team in Chicago, and I'll get back to you within the week. You realize nothing will happen until the spring because of the weather?"

"We do, but we want to get a head start."

"Why do you want this so badly?"

Jurgens blew out a breath. "The helmet is special, but the chest is supposed to have an abundance of pieces that will explain Viking history, and that's what we're looking for. There are items in there that show how they lived. And of course, the coins will help us finance other projects. But this is our first major project. It'll get us started."

"I understand."

"Please join us tonight at a social event here at the office. Can you make it?"

"I'm free all day and night."

Drexel nodded. "Let's show you around then. "The two men took Wil on a tour of other places of interest to them and returned to the office around six for the social event. The party was already in full swing with about twenty people milling around with drinks in hand.

A man joined Wil immediately. "You're Wil Bolton. We've heard all about you and wanted to pick your brain on the Papua New Guinea find."

"I'll answer what I can."

Another guy joined them and took out a pad of paper. "What amazed you about the find?"

Wil frowned. "Are you two reporters?"

"Guilty," one laughed.

"Then it's best you talk to Mr. Loe."

"Can we just ask you a few questions?"

"Sorry." Wil walked away and spent another hour

mingling before he had enough and went to tell Drexel and Jurgens goodbye. "I have an early plane flight, so I'm heading back to the hotel."

"We'll get someone to give you a ride."

"Wonderful." Wil made it back to the hotel and filled the hot tub. He had no sooner jumped in when his cell phone vibrated.

"Uncle Wil where have you been? We've missed you."

"I've missed you also, Maddie."

"When will you be home?"

"Probably Wednesday or Thursday. I'm in New York City right now."

"We're going to have to put something on you to keep track of you. Here's Jonathan. He has a question for you."

A little boy's voice piped in. "When you get back, will you grill with me?"

"You bet I will."

"Great. Here's Mom."

"Hey, Wil. The kids were dying to talk to you. How are things going?"

"Busy. I'm here in New York City learning all I can about Viking history."

"That's interesting. Are you going to Norway next?"

"No, actually these sites are located in North America, but then again who knows where we'll be off to. They've also talked about Africa, probably one of those blasted countries that hates America."

"That seems to be where all the treasures are. Is everything okay with you?"

"Why do you ask?"

"I got a call from Kelsey a week or so ago, and she explained to me what had happened with everything, and she really seemed sincere about it. I was just wondering if you had talked to her."

"I told her we were through. Now I need to go. The water in the hot tub is getting cold."

Chapter 31

Wil landed back in Chicago Thursday afternoon. He took a cab to Mr. Loe's office for their meeting. There were two other gentlemen waiting when he entered.

Mr. Loe stood. "Come on in, Wil. Tell us what you found out."

"You'll enjoy it."

"I bet you we will. These are two of my closest advisors on treasures and artifacts. We're just having a discussion on where we're going next. Let's see what you have."

Wil laid out the information on a large table in Mr. Loe's office. "Here are some books and papers on the Viking helmet that the group is looking for. It is actually their first expedition. If they're successful, they plan to join your group in the future, which is a good thing."

"It is," Mr. Loe said. "What else did you find out?"

"They've narrowed the location of this helmet to three spots: Minnesota, Maine, and Newfoundland. What's more exciting is that the guys at Archaeological Synopsis believe there is a treasure hidden with the helmet that holds items that tell the Vikings story in

America."

All three of the men raised their eyes. "That is amazing," Mr. Loe said. "When can we get started?"

"Probably best to start in the spring because the winter weather will make it difficult, plus there's paperwork that needs to be gathered. Also, I wanted to share one other thing with you, Mr. Loe. And I'd like to do it in private."

Mr. Loe nodded his head for the other two to leave his office. He shut the door and turned to Wil. "What is going on?"

"I've decided I'm going back to my cabin and figure out where I'm going in life."

"I thought this is what you wanted."

"I enjoy the adventure, but I also really care about Kelsey, and I want to see if we can make something of our lives together."

"Kelsey is right here, and she knows what is happening."

"I'm just not sure where the two of us our heading at this point, and I need to figure it out before I make any other commitments in my life."

Mr. Loe stuck out his hand. "I can understand, and I want you to know that whenever you're ready, you'll always have a job here. In fact, I have your first commission check."

He went back to his desk and handed Wil a check.

Wil's jaw dropped. "That's two million dollars, Mr. Loe. How much did you make off of this?"

Mr. Loe grinned. "Close to twenty-million dollars with the money we received from the Lawrences."

"I don't understand."

"Easy, Lawrence and I always split everything

fifty-fifty. That's the deal we made to stay out of each other's hair."

Wil just shook his head. "Businessmen."

~

Wil flew back to South Dakota and arrived at his cabin later that day. Over the next two weeks, everything was quiet in Wil's life. He hadn't heard from Kelsey, but then again, she had told him it was up to him to make the first move about their relationship. He glanced down at his cell phone when it vibrated.

"How are things in South Dakota?" Mr. Loe asked.

"The weather is starting to get cold, and winter is on its way."

"I know what you mean. We're gearing up for a trip to Africa to look for artifacts dealing with the Romans. Are you interested?"

"I appreciate the offer, but I'm going to pass until I can get myself together. It's coming along."

"That's good to hear. Kelsey has broken everything off with her family. She moved out of the mansion and is renting her own place."

Silence ensued, then Boris spoke. "Wil, I'm not asking for any commitments, but why don't you fly out to Chicago this weekend and spend some time in the Windy City? There is a major convention this weekend that my wife and I will attend that may interest you."

"What kind of convention?"

"A clothing and design convention."

Wil laughed. "I could understand your wife checking it out, but that's nothing I could imagine you participating in."

"People from all over the world attend, and who knows? Maybe you'll connect with someone that interests you."

Wil was quiet. "Why not? If nothing else, I can check out the latest fashions. Yuck."

"And see Kelsey Lawrence."

"It won't happen."

Boris Loe was waiting for Wil at the O'Hare International Airport when he landed the next afternoon.

"Good to see you, Wil. Let's grab a bite to eat at Harry Caray's, and I have something to show you after. Harry Caray's has always been a cool place because it's filled with baseball memorabilia."

Wil nodded. "I remember watching Cubs games and him, and he was always singing, 'Take Me out to the Ball Game.'"

"Yeah, people are fascinated with their Cubs here in Chicago."

The server joined them.

"What would you like to eat?"

Wil quickly surveyed the menu. "The Italian beef sandwich with potato wedges and a glass of water is fine."

The two chatted as they ate. An hour later they drove down to McCormick Place. Boris parked the car, and they ambled toward the facility.

Wil stopped and stared up at the building with its open space and state-of-the-art design. "This is so cool."

Boris smiled. "It is considered the largest convention center in North America. There are four interconnected buildings and one indoor area near the shore of Lake Michigan. It hosts trade shows and conferences. Part of it was also used as a makeshift hospital during the pandemic."

The two walked inside and Wil was thrilled once more. "Look at how open this place is."

"There are more than two million square feet of exhibit space and more than one million square feet on one level. This is the first time the clothing and design group has held the annual convention in this place in the six years Kelsey has been operating the business."

"So she didn't sell the business after all," he said.

The two walked over to where people had set up booths and displays. Wil stopped and noticed Kelsey, helping a couple of ladies. She was dressed in a sweater, with sweatpants, and her hair up in a ponytail. Wil and Boris stood for a moment watching the group.

"She will always love you, Wil."

Wil snapped out of his trance and turned to Boris. "It'll never work because we're too different."

"Maybe. Let's join her. She's going to give us a tour."

Kelsey smiled when she saw him, but didn't act surprised. She showed them around the facility, ever the businesswoman. It was around four when Boris and he walked toward the car.

Boris stopped before he opened his car door. "There's a ticket waiting for you if you decide to attend tonight's festivities. You may enjoy it because Kelsey will give a speech on how she landed the Brazil deal. Wil, it's the first American clothing and design business that has penetrated the Brazilian market."

Chapter 32

Wil decided to attend the conference at the last minute. After he entered the convention center, he grabbed a glass of wine and surveyed the area. He finally saw Kelsey talking to a couple near one of the clothing booths. She was dressed in a one-piece, strapless blue dress, with what looked like three-inch heels. Her hair was frosted with light blonde tones mixed in with her normal brown hair. This was the most beautiful Wil had ever seen her.

"Little brother, what are you doing here?" Carly hurried over pulling on Cole's arm.

"Cole, Carly, it's good to see you once again."

Cole laughed. "Are you being sarcastic? We both know we can't stand each other."

"That's true but I am surprised Carly is still with you. She either hasn't figured out who you really are at this point, or she likes who you are."

Cole glared at him. "She knows exactly who I am, and she adores being with me. Isn't that right, dear?"

Carly shrugged. "Wil, what are you doing here?"

Wil sighed. "Checking on whether my brother is involved in distributing drugs and diamonds through clothing."

Cole laughed. "Yeah, right. I would never do anything like that."

Wil rolled his eyes. "I should probably get a refill on my drink."

"You do that," Cole said. "Like always, it's good to see you."

Wil watched as the two disappeared. He turned at a tap on his shoulder.

"Wil Bolton, it's great to see you once more, although I'm surprised you'd be here at this event after what my daughter did to you."

"Mr. Lawrence, we both know Kelsey did what she had to do to help her family because that's what family does."

Hank grinned. "You understand the concept of family, and that's a good thing."

Wil sighed. "What I can't understand is why you are even here. There is no gold in any of these items."

Hank looked at him confused. "What do you mean?"

"There must be something else in the clothes industry that you're interested in. Say, drugs? Or even diamonds?"

Mr. Lawrence laughed. "That's as far-fetched an idea as I've ever heard. How would we get these through customs? It isn't possible."

"Simple because you have all the money you need to get it done, and we both know money allows people to look the other way."

"I'm sorry, but you're wrong. I'm an honest businessman," he said, sipping his Champagne.

"That is good to know. I'll be able to rest easier."

"I hear you're a big Knicks fan."

"You must have been misinformed. I'm from South Dakota, and we either cheer for Denver or Minnesota sports teams. I'm partial to Denver because it's closer."

"I must have been misinformed."

"It sounds like it. Are you a Bears ticket holder?"

"We're there for every home game. You should join us for this Sunday's home game in our box suites. All the food and drink you can handle."

"I'll think about it."

"You do that. We'll chat some more."

Wil found a place in the back to sit and listen to Kelsey's presentation about her company with Roberto Santiago in Brazil. Kelsey's mother sat down next to him.

"Good to see you, Mr. Bolton. I'm surprised you're still around my daughter after what she did to you."

"We're not together," Wil said.

"That's good to hear. All you would do is destroy her future. She and her father are tight. She was able to start her business because of the funding her father provided her. She's never forgotten that."

Wil frowned. "What you're saying is she does your husband's bidding?"

The woman shook her head. "I wouldn't call it that. It's called being a family, and the Lawrences are a family. Kelsey moved out of her home for one reason, and that was to move closer to you. But it's not what you think — it was for her father and for profit. Kelsey is incredibly good at what she does."

Wil stood. Anything to get away from this evil woman.

She sipped her drink. "You've met some of her

boyfriends, and she has all of them under her thumb. Why do you think she wears such intimate clothes in the middle of winter? It's for luring young men like yourself into her web of deceit, and she's exceptionally good at it. I should know because I taught her everything she knows."

Wil took a deep breath. "You're wrong about this one. Kelsey actually does care about a certain guy and wants to start her own life away from you and her father and the rest of the Lawrence contingent."

Kelsey's mom laughed lightly. "And lose more than two million dollars a year she can use for whatever she wants? I don't think so, and especially not with someone like you."

"Why are you telling me all of this?"

"Good question. If you think you're going to woo her away into your arms and marry her, forget it."

She rose to her full height and pointed a manicured finger at his chest. "It's time you realized that she and Nolan Gant have been promised to each other since they were in high school. Kelsey has had tons of boyfriends, but in the end, she always comes back to Nolan. That'll never change." She glanced up at the front. "Oh look, Kelsey is starting her presentation. This should be quite interesting."

Throughout the day, Wil stayed away from Kelsey so she could do her thing. What her mother told him unsettled him. He didn't believe what she said, but with what had happened in the past, who knew what was true?

After the presentation Wil wandered around the convention floor and had just noticed a booth from India when Carly came up beside him.

"You're still here?"

"Yeah, I'm not sure why I'm still here. What about you?"

"Cole had some business he needed to conduct with the Lawrences, so I'm just hanging out until he's finished. Do you want to join me for a drink?"

"Why not? I could do with a drink."

The two headed over to the bar, grabbed a table, and they both ordered beers. While they were waiting, they watched people browse the various kiosks.

"I can't believe how popular this has become," Carly said.

"Have you been to this convention before?"

"Last year I went with Cole. He goes to these clothing events around the country."

Wil sipped his beer. "I can't remember Cole ever being into fashion of any kind."

Carly shook her head. "The last couple of years he started going to these things. You know he works for Mr. Lawrence, or more specifically for Kelsey Lawerence?"

"Kelsey?"

"Oh yes, Cole's been on her payroll for the past couple of years. He and I visit these different clothing and design conventions to find new styles and pass them along to Kelsey."

"Is that all you do?"

"What do you mean?"

"If you're looking at clothes together, why are you here by yourself?"

"Like I said, Wil, he has some business he needs to do with Mr. Lawrence. Hank or his brother, Ben, are usually at these events in support of Kelsey. You don't realize how close this whole family is, and that includes the mother and siblings." Carly took a sip of her beer. "You're nothing like your brothers. Why is that?"

Wil shook his head. "I took a different path because I didn't like what my family does. My two brothers were always in some kind of trouble, so I stayed away. You should think about doing the same thing."

Carly smiled. "Sorry, Wil, Cole and I plan to get married next summer. I hope you come to the wedding."

"It's hard to imagine Cole marrying anybody."

"That's funny because he says the same thing about you, and as I told you, Kelsey has ulterior motives for everything that she does. If you think she loves you, there's a good chance she wants something from you. What it is you'll never know until it's too late. So, you should rethink what you're doing also."

"Maybe. Tell me, why do you love my brother? Or do you even love Cole?"

Carly shrugged. "That's a good question. Probably because he takes the time to be with me. No guy has ever shown me he cares like Cole does."

"That's what I don't understand. You're a beautiful woman who can have any guy you want, but you're settling for my brother. Then you say I don't know Kelsey, but it's a good bet you don't know Cole or my family. Be careful."

Once she left, Wil checked out the rest of the convention. Kelsey was talking to Holloman and Cole, and Wil wondered what was up. He approached where they were standing so he could hear what they were saying.

"Carly is getting way too nosy," Cole said. "I'm not sure if we can trust her anymore."

Kelsey glared at him. "You know what to do. Why didn't you take care of it in Papua?"

"Not with Wil there. You told me nothing must happen to him, and she was right next to him. I couldn't take a chance."

"Yeah, that would make sense."

Holloman joined in. "Kelsey, how long is this charade going to go on with the two of you?"

"You don't believe I could fall in love with Wil?"

Holloman laughed. "Not in our lifetime."

Kelsey sighed. "I'll use him as long as I need to. The Africa trip is a big one, and we have to capitalize on it, then everything will be ours for the taking."

"I don't know if he'll be going," Cole said.

Kelsey sighed. "Everyone has a price. Find out what it is."

Chapter 33

That evening as part of the clothing event there was a social banquet with food, music, and dancing. Wil arrived around eight and grabbed a glass of wine. He surveyed the large banquet room and saw the Loes talking to a couple of people he had seen before but couldn't recall who they were.

Mrs. Loe noticed him and gestured for Wil to join her. "Good to see you, Wil. I'm glad you made it. I'd like you to meet someone who's been dying to meet you." She took his hand and pulled him to a couple of gals standing with Mr. Loe and another guy. "Wil, I'd like you to meet my sister, Nadia, who's visiting from New York City. She's asked about you a couple of times since she's been here."

Nadia rolled her eyes. "Big sister, like usual you're exaggerating."

"You said you wanted to meet him."

"I never said that. I just mentioned to my friend that he looked handsome, but so do several other guys I've seen tonight."

Boris laughed. "Wil, Nadia came to Chicago because her sister said there were much better-looking guys here than in New York."

Wil scratched his head. "That's hard to imagine considering New York City has ten million more people than Chicago in their respective metro areas."

Nadia grinned. "Wow, not only handsome but smart. Are you sure no one has snatched him up yet?"

Mrs. Loe shook his head. "One gal has tried her best, but they can't seem to get it together."

"And who might that be?" Nadia asked.

"In fact, she's right there," Mrs. Loe said, pointing to Kelsey who was with Brandon.

"Kelsey Lawrence wouldn't think about Wil unless she needed something from him."

"You know this how?" Boris asked.

"Simple," Nadia said. "She's a Lawrence, and they're like royalty, meaning only men of significant means can marry or associate with them. Wil hardly qualifies."

Wil laughed. "I see you've already judged me, ma'am. That must make you not too different from Ms. Lawrence." Wil turned to the Loes. "I should get going. It was good to see you, Mrs. Loe." He caught a taxi to the pier, then sat down on one of the benches overlooking Lake Michigan and stared out at the waves beating against the sand. What was he doing here? Was it the lure of the treasure hunt or Kelsey?

"I thought I saw you earlier tonight at the convention. What are you doing here?"

He peered up at Kelsey who sat down next to him on the bench. "That's the question I've been trying to answer myself."

"What have you figured out?"

Wil laughed. "Nothing."

"Maybe I can help you. Was it because you were

looking for new clothes or the gals who model them?”
She grinned.

He shrugged. “Or it was Mr. Loe who continues to
hound me about going on this treasure-hunting
expedition to Africa.”

“I thought you gave all that adventure up?”

“Yeah, but every time he calls, he produces
something that makes me think about it. The clothing
and design conference was a way for me to meet
contacts, he said. I met a few people including your
mother, my brother, Cole, and Mrs. Loe’s sister. What a
treat!”

Kelsey laughed. “What happened?”

“Mrs. Loe’s sister, Nadia, told me I’m only good
enough to be your servant, so basically I’m out of your
league, which I had already figured out.”

Kelsey moaned. “That bitch. I’ve never considered
you a servant. And…”

“Cole isn’t into clothes, but he’s up to something
with your father and uncle. One thing I do know is Cole
has always been into drugs, so it’s interesting to find
out Cole is on your payroll.”

Kelsey’s face turned red.

“Wow, you have a known drug dealer on your
payroll, so it makes me think you knew all along that
your father was smuggling drugs and diamonds in your
‘fashion and design’ business.”

“It’s not what you think. I will explain to you
what’s happening if you give me a chance.”

“I’m not going anywhere.”

Kelsey stared out into the water. “Cole knows a lot
about his little brother, and I wanted information about
you to help me do what I needed to do. I knew about his

drug dealings. but the only thing I received from him was information about you. That's the truth."

Wil eyed her. "And your mother was the icing on the cake."

"I can imagine." Kelsey rolled her eyes.

"She told me you lure every man into your 'web of deceit' with your sexy clothing, and I'm just another of those men you've used to get what you wanted. I did piss her off by telling her there is a guy out there that you actually do care about."

She took Wil's hands. "There is. You have changed how I feel about everything."

Wil glared at Kelsey. "How can I trust you? It's time to stop this charade. You have no feelings for me. You're just using me."

"It's not like that at all."

He pulled away from her. "Isn't it? I heard you talking to Cole and Holloman about Carly, about me."

She glared at him. "I was lying to them to protect you, Wil."

"Protect me? That's a crock, and you know it. Once you get what you need, there will be no me, and we both know that."

"You're way wrong, Wil. I am in love with you, but it's not as easy as you make it out to be. I am still a Lawrence and I have to play this role they expect—to be evil and manipulative, so yes, I used to be a bitch who took advantage of others. That was what I was supposed to do, and I did my job. But I've regretted it ever since I met you." She took Wil's hands. "You have changed how I feel about everything. I miss you every day, and I worry about you when you're gone. When we make love with each other, it's like we're in another world. None of this true love stuff has happened to me before you — ever." She tried to calm down her breathing. "Don't tell me you've never done anything that you regret."

"Of course, I have, but what you've done has gone way overboard, dictating who lives and who dies."

"Damn it, Wil, I was just trying to protect you. Don't sit on your high horse and say you're this perfect angel. You're not."

He stared at her. "You and I will never be. I'm flying back to South Dakota in the morning, so you go back and tell your family they can go to hell because I'm through. And this time for good."

Kelsey glared at him. "No, Wil, it's not over because you showed up here, and it shows me you do care about our relationship. I asked you to take the lead."

"I tried to, but I wasn't getting anywhere. You're too enmeshed in evil."

"You're right. It's going to take time. I'm not giving up on us, and I hope you won't either."

Wil took a deep breath. "Why do you continue to do all this? Why can't you just walk away from it?"

"Do what?"

"If you don't know, I can't begin to tell you."

She took his head gently into his hands and kissed him. "I'm playing two roles. Don't trust what you hear; trust what we have."

~

Wil had just prepared to board the plane when he stopped and noticed a tall guy coming off the plane. He had seen him twice before, and both times there had preceded a death soon after. It was quite a coincidence that he would show up each time. Who was he?

Wil shrugged it off and ambled onto the flight headed back to Rapid City. He arrived back in Rapid City around four in the afternoon. Since it was the middle of December, it was snowing like usual. The weather forecaster predicted a major blizzard in the southern Black Hills over the next couple of days.

Wil's drive was easy until he reached Nemo Road, and then the drive became more treacherous because of the heavy snow and the increased winds. He finally made it back to his cabin three hours after he left Rapid City, a trip that usually lasted ninety minutes. He had just sat down on his couch when his cell phone vibrated.

"Are you home, Uncle Wil? Are you safe?"

"I just got home, Maddie. I'm okay."

"Oh good. Everything is closed around here, and Mom said you were just coming back from Chicago. What were you doing in Chicago? Did you get to see Kelsey?"

"I saw Kelsey, but I'm not going to tell you what we did."

Maddie laughed. "I'm sure you kissed her. I saw Mom kissing the deputy sheriff the other night."

"Maddie, that's enough." Tessa came on the line. "And she's only eleven," Tessa sighed. "I'm glad you're back okay."

"It took three hours to reach the cabin."

"Why didn't you just stay in Rapid?"

"And miss the adventure of the drive down Nemo Road?"

Tessa laughed. "Yeah, it gets crazy on that road. How's Chicago? Did I hear Maddie say you kissed

Kelsey? Never mind, I can't keep up with you."

"What's this about you and the deputy sheriff?"

She blew out a breath. "It's happening faster than I would like it to. He's a nice guy and sweet towards Maddie and Jonathan, but I'm not sure."

"You deserve happiness."

"And so do you, Wil. Kelsey loves you."

"And I love her, but we can't be together because of her family."

"She loves you enough to break away from them."

"I don't think she will."

Chapter 34

The blizzard continued for two days in the Black Hills. Wil's scanner said that the state had closed down all the roads in the Black Hills and closed down Interstate 90 from the Wyoming border to Chamberlain along the Missouri River. It was a normal occurrence in South Dakota.

What was also a normal occurrence was people traveling along roads that were impassable. It was after four the next day when his cell phone rang. "Hello, Sheriff."

"Wil, can you get out of your cabin?"

"I should be able to."

"We have a couple and their two kids stranded along Highway 385 just off the Sheridan Lake Road. The plows can't get out, but the family contacted us and said they are low on petrol and food. Can you make it out there?"

"That'll be tough. You know how bad it gets in that area."

"I know, but our department is crazy with others stuck right outside of Rapid City."

"Okay, I'm on my way." Wil clicked off his cell phone, gathered his winter gear, some food for the family, blankets to keep them warm, and gas for their vehicle. He climbed into his four-wheel-drive pickup which had always been high enough to get through any blizzard to date in the Black Hills.

The drive toward Highway 385 was slow going, and the roads were treacherous in places, but he pulled out of it. It took him an hour to reach Highway 385, then he headed toward Hill City. He finally found Sheridan Lake Road, made a slow turn on the road, and saw the vehicle stuck in a snowbank.

He pulled to the side and hurried out to see what could be done. He tried the doors, but they were frozen shut. He wiped away some snow and saw the family. The parents, a little boy, and a girl. They didn't look like they were alive.

Wil hurried around to the back window and broke through, then pried one of the back doors open and was able to get the little girl out. She couldn't be any more than Maddie's age, but she was barely alive. He scrambled with her over to the pickup and placed her in it, covering her up the best he could.

He grabbed the phone and called the sheriff's department, who answered immediately.

"Wil, how is it?" the sheriff asked.

"The little girl is still alive, but I don't know if the others are going to make it. They need help."

"We can't get there, Wil. Do what you can to take them to the Monument Health Clinic in Hill City. They've been helpful in the past and are aware of the situation."

"Okay." Wil went back and pulled the boy out of the back of the car but couldn't find a pulse. He hustled back to the truck and placed him with his sister. The hard part was pulling the parents out.

It was a struggle but he was finally able to carry them to the pickup. It was a tight squeeze, but Wil placed the kids on top of their parents and wrapped them up the best he could. He grabbed the cell phone.

"We're on our way. Other than the little girl, I don't know if any are alive."

"Bring them here and we'll do what we can. A doctor is already there and waiting for you. We've found out that they're traveling from Chicago to Los Angeles and got lost coming out of Rapid City."

"How do you know that?"

"They told us when they called 9-1-1. Wil, they have no family."

Wil slowly made his way toward Hill City. It took him close to an hour to get there. A nurse and the doctor helped Wil transfer the family into the clinic. Wil dropped down on a seat and waited to see what became of the family.

Several hours later the doctor came out and sat down by Wil.

"You saved the little girl's life, and the mother is hanging on, barely. The other two didn't make it."

"What will happen to the little girl?"

"That's a good question. The sheriff's department has been trying to find relatives, but so far no luck."

"How is the little girl doing?"

"She's suffered frostbite and hypothermia, but she'll make it, Wil, because you wrapped her in that blanket in a warm car." The doctor took a deep breath. "The mother is close to dying, but she wanted to talk to the man who saved her daughter's life."

Wil looked at her. "What can I do?"

"Just listen to her. My guess is she's providing her last testament and wants you to hear it."

Wil took a deep breath and walked into the room. The gal was barely awake and covered with tubes. She opened her eyes when he walked in. "Please sit down by me," she whispered.

Wil pulled up a chair and took her hand. "Thank you for saving my baby. We were so stupid to even try leaving Rapid City, but my husband had to make sure we reached Deadwood where we had reservations at a hotel. I'm not going to make it, but I want you to look after Abigail. She has no family left."

"None?" Wil said, glancing up at the doctor.

"No one. All four of her grandparents have died over the last five years. We're both only children. My last hope is that someone would watch over her, and you braved this blizzard to save her life. Please take care of her, and don't let anything happen to her. Then I can die in peace."

Wil started to speak once more, but the lines on the machines coalesced into a straight, horizontal line. He jumped back as the doctor and a nurse hurried to try to get her heart started once more. A few minutes later, the doctor glanced at the clock. "Time of death, eleven-twelve p.m."

Wil slowly walked out to the waiting room and plopped down on a bench. He didn't know why he did it, but he hit Kelsey's number.

She answered after the second ring. "Wil, are you okay?"

"They're dead. I couldn't save them, and they froze to death."

"Your sister and the kids?"

"No, another family was stuck in the blizzard. They froze to death, except for the little girl who has no family. Her mother's dying wish was for me to watch over her. I can't handle myself. How am I supposed to handle a ten-year-old?"

"Wil, I'll fly out there first thing in the morning."

"No, don't."

"I want to. I have to. I need to hold you and make sure you're okay."

"I should have never called you. We can't be together, and we both know it'll never work because your family won't let you leave."

Chapter 35

Wil drank coffee and remained in the waiting room of the Monument Hospital in Rapid City. Abigail had been transferred to the hospital two days earlier and had been there for four days now. Tessa and the kids had stopped by the day before to make sure he was okay and bring him fresh clothes.

One of the nurses stepped out. "Little Abigail is awake and is asking for you."

Wil looked at her. "Does she know?"

The nurse took a deep breath. "Abigail knew it in the car. She tried to keep them going."

"How is she going to ever live past that?"

"It'll be hard, but she has a tough-minded guy to help her."

Wil looked confused. The nurse smiled. "Maddie tells my daughter all about her Uncle Wil, and how much he's done for her and Jonathan."

"Got ya."

"I do have some good news. The sheriff's department found an aunt who is on her way today to pick her up and take her home."

"That's wonderful news."

"She would like to meet you."

Wil walked slowly into the room. The young girl looked up and smiled through watery eyes. "Thank you, sir, for trying to save my parents and my brother. You couldn't do anything because they were dead, and I couldn't do anything to help them."

"You did all you could. It was the blizzard's fault."

"No, my dad should have never left Rapid City. He and my mom argued. They argued all the time."

"I'm sorry to hear that. Good news is your aunt will pick you up and take you home."

Abigail stared at him. "My mom and dad have no relatives. I have no aunt."

He frowned. "Are you sure?"

"I am sure. My mom and dad didn't have any sisters or brothers, and my grandparents are dead."

"Maybe some other relative?"

"No. My mom talked many times about wishing she had relatives, but she didn't have any."

Wil took a deep breath. "You had better get some sleep."

Abigail took his hand. "Please don't leave me."

"I'll sit right here."

The little girl held onto his hand until she fell asleep. Wil dialed the sheriff's office.

"Wil, is the little girl okay?"

"Sheriff, she's fine, but she's telling me she doesn't have any relatives, and supposedly an aunt is on her way here to pick her up."

"Do you know who the little girl is?"

"Of course, I don't."

"Sorry, but she's the heir to a multi-million-dollar fortune."

"Are you kidding me?"

"I'm not. Their attorneys found a will that turns all the money over to the surviving children, and it doesn't list anyone as a relative. In fact, the will states that the grandparents are the only relatives."

"What happens to the little girl?"

"Legally, she'll have to go to Social Services unless we can figure out a way for someone to take custody of her."

Wil sighed. "Tessa?"

The sheriff responded. "What about your sister?"

"She can take her and will take her."

"I'll get right on it," the sheriff said. "I'll contact the judge and get him to stop any transfer until things are sorted out."

The next day the judge ordered that Tessa, if she consented to it, would have temporary custody of the child until it was proven that the lady who arrived was her aunt.

Wil was sitting out front with Abigail at his sister's house waiting for her aunt to show up.

"I hoped I could stay with you," the little girl said.

"Abigail, you'll be better off with your aunt. And she is your aunt."

"Why did my mom and dad lie?"

"I can't answer that. That's something you'll have to talk to your aunt about."

"That's the first thing I'll do."

They turned as a vehicle pulled up. A man and lady who looked in their early forties climbed out of a Bentley. "Abigail, it is you?" the lady said. She started to hug her, but Abigail pushed her away.

"I've never met you before."

The lady stepped back. "You wouldn't remember

me because your mom and dad decided I shouldn't be included with your family. I'm your mother's sister, and we had a big fight when we were younger. This is my husband, and he wanted to come and meet you also."

The man peered at Abigail. "You've grown up some. Here, let me show you some of your photos when you're younger."

The man lifted Abigail on the hood of the car and went through photos. The lady turned to Wil. "Thank you for saving at least one of them. My sister was always stubborn, but her husband was even worse. My sister and I had a major fight over the guy she married."

The lady turned to look at Abigail, then turned back to Wil. "Please give me your phone number so if Abigail ever needs to talk to you for any reason, she can. She'll never forget what you've done for her, and I want to make sure she has someone she can trust. It'll take a while for her to trust my husband and me."

~

It was a week before Christmas and Tessa had called Wil to tell him that she and the kids were going to join the deputy sheriff in Arizona for Christmas with his family.

"You're really getting serious, Tessa?"

"I am," she agreed. "He's been so beautiful toward the kids, and they enjoy their time with him. I hope you're okay with what's happening."

"Of course, I am."

"I'm just sorry we can't spend Christmas with you, but you have always loved your peaceful little cabin for Christmas."

"That's true." As soon as he hung up the call from

Tessa, his phone vibrated, so he pulled over to the side of the road and picked it up.

"Wil, how are you doing?"

"Mr. Hampton, I'm doing well. What can I do for you?"

"You remember the guy at Ditch Creek Road?"

"Yep. Did he shoot another mountain lion?"

"This time a coyote, or I should say two coyotes. He shot them dead, but he also was wounded in the engagement."

"What?"

"It sounds like it was a pack of coyotes. We have the forest-service reps heading that way, but I thought you'd be able to help them out a bit."

"I'll drive over there and see what I can do."

Wil arrived at the place thirty minutes later and found the EMTs with the old man. Wil knelt down by him.

"I got two of them rascals. but there were just too many of them."

"How many?"

"At least six coyotes."

"What would bring them up here?"

"I don't know."

The deputy sheriff joined Wil and the guy. "Where did you get all those cats back there?"

The man shrugged, then winced from the pain. "They just wander back here, knowing that I'll take care of them."

The deputy eyed him. "You need to start telling me the truth. You're stealing them, aren't you?"

The men hesitated. "Damn it, Deputy, most of those cats are strays or neglected by their families. They try to escape, and I capture them and bring them here. Why is that an issue?"

"How many cats do you believe you have out there, and how do you feed them?"

"There's probably a hundred cats back there, and I feed them what I can. At least that's my goal. Again, what's the problem with taking care of the cats?"

The deputy sighed. "Do you realize having too many cats increases the risk of transmitting disease? How do you keep up with treatment and routine vaccinations?"

"There is no need. They're feral cats. If not, I assume their previous owners gave them all the treatment they needed."

The deputy finished writing down notes and looked up once more. "You realize not only do they spread disease among the cats, they also can transmit diseases to humans, which would mean you."

The guy winced. "I've been itching a lot, and it seems like I have diarrhea, and that really stinks."

The deputy took another breath. "Sir, it's also a reason the mountain lion and the coyotes today are becoming more prevalent at your cabin. They have a food source."

"Then I'll keep killing them if I have to."

"No, sir, we're going to do something about it. We'll round up the cats, and we're going to get you the treatment you need. No questions asked."

The man fumed at the deputy then started coughing.

Chapter 36

"I'm surprised to hear from you, Mr. Loe," Wil said.

Boris laughed. "I'm a persistent kind of guy and will keep discussing the Africa trip with you."

"I thought you would have gone by now."

"If you're not busy, why don't you join the family for Christmas this year? Then afterwards we'll get cracking on forming the new team unless you have other plans?"

"No, I don't. My sister is going to Arizona with her boyfriend. She has the right idea."

"I agree there. Can I count on you?"

"I'll be there."

It was Saturday when Wil climbed on the plane. One of the flight attendants smiled at him. "Welcome aboard, Mr. Bolton."

Wil laughed. "I've flown too much to Chicago."

"You have," she laughed. "I remember many of our regular passengers. Are you off to Chicago to celebrate Christmas?"

"Yeah."

"I hope you enjoy yourself."

"How about you?"

She smiled. "Christmas in Chicago also."

"Enjoy yourself."

It was three days before Christmas when Wil strolled into his hotel. A major snowstorm had blanketed Chicago the night before, which made it difficult to get around. It was Saturday night and Wil decided to head downtown to a couple of nightclubs.

He hadn't sat down for more than five minutes at the first bar when a familiar gal walked up to him. They both laughed.

"I see you're preparing for Christmas." the flight attendant said.

"Seems like you are also."

"We are. Would you like to join us?"

"Why not?"

"By the way, my name is Salome."

"I remember that from your name tag."

She gently hit her head. "True. Don't be too freaked out by my friends. We've been buddies since grade school."

"I'm good."

Wil stayed with them for about ninety minutes, then he headed down the street to another nightclub. He walked in and noticed right away it was much more crowded than the first one.

"Oh my gosh, Wil Bolton. What are you doing here?"

Wil turned to Alexis and JJ who had walked in behind him. "I decided to check out the night scene."

"No date tonight?" JJ asked.

"Sorry, I didn't pack one in my suitcase."

JJ laughed. "I always liked your sense of humor. We may have the perfect gal for you tonight. Sorry it's not Kelsey, although she'll be here tonight with her new boyfriend. His name is Brandon Drury or something like that."

"Brandon Roble and he's a banking president. Kelsey's type of guy with lots of money."

"That's true. She does like handsome guys with money, but then she seemed to care about you much more than most any other guy she's been with," JJ said.

Wil ignored the comment. "Is Brandon from Colorado?"

JJ nodded. "How would you know that?"

Wil laughed. "Just a lucky guess."

"You'll have to let us in on the secret," Alexis said. "Let's find a table. Lisa will be here soon with Clinton. The two have been dating since they returned from South Dakota."

They found a table away from the crowded area, and a few moments later, Clinton and Lisa joined them. Once Lisa saw Wil, she gave him a hug and kiss on the cheek. She turned to Clinton who had followed behind. "I'm dumping you for Wil tonight."

Everyone laughed. Clinton took Wil's hand and shook it. "Good to see you, my friend."

"You too. I hear you two are seeing each other."

Lisa grinned. "We're going to be married in January, and we're expecting our first child in April."

"Congratulations." Wil said.

They all turned to a gal who had bumped into Clinton. She said her apologies, then stopped when she saw Wil and they both laughed.

"You two know each other?" Alexis asked.

"Yep, he's a regular flier on my flight from Rapid City to Chicago," Salome said.

"I'll be darned," JJ said. "This works out perfectly. Wil, since you're the new guy, you buy the first rounds."

Wil grinned. "I can handle it."

He bought everyone a round and left two beers for Brandon and Kelsey when he heard they were coming.

~

The minute Kelsey noticed the others, took Brandon's hand, and joined them.

"Hey, Kelsey. We have a surprise for you." Alexis said and pointed to Wil and Salome who were dancing on the floor.

Brandon frowned. "Is that Wil Bolton?"

Kelsey stared at Brandon. "You know him?"

"Yes, his sister, Tessa, works with me in the banking industry. We both started in Washington. She moved to Deadwood to be closer to Wil, and I decided to relocate to Chicago."

She glared at him. "That's why you didn't say anything when he showed up at my condo?"

"What was there to say? We both know that Wil isn't the guy for you. You deserve much better than him, and now I'm here, so it makes it a moot point."

JJ handed the two each a beer. "Wil bought the first round."

Kelsey unscrewed the cap off her beer and looked at Wil, her heart racing. What was he doing here? And she was with Brandon. This wasn't going to be a good night. After a couple of dances, Wil and Salome joined the others.

"Brandon, good to see you," Wil said, shaking his hand.

"You too. How's Tessa?"

"Doing well. She's on her way to Arizona to spend Christmas with a deputy sheriff and left me hanging."

Brandon laughed. "You always told her you preferred your cabin during Christmas because you didn't have to be around anyone."

"True, but Mr. Loe invited me here and wanted me to help him with a project, so here I am."

"Why don't you join the rest of us for a Christmas Eve party downtown? You'll love it. I'm sure Salome would join us also."

"I'd love to," Salome said.

"You know her?"

Brandon nodded. "You're not the only one who flies the friendly skies."

"Got ya."

Kelsey touched Wil's hand, and her eyes pleaded with him. "I love this song. Will you dance with me?"

Wil glanced at Brandon. "Do you mind?"

"Of course not, I'm not too worried about you, Wil. Kelsey has better taste than that." He laughed.

Kelsey grabbed Wil's hand, led him to the dance floor, and wrapped her arms around his neck. "What are you doing here at this nightclub tonight?"

"I told you Boris asked me to join him for Christmas, and the reason I came to this nightclub was I decided to check out the nightlife in Chicago."

"And you just happened to remember I'm here on a Saturday night?"

Wil grinned. "Of course, I did."

"Damn you, why are you doing this to me?"

"Doing what?"

"Coming to Chicago when I'm with another guy, and not telling me you're going to be here at this nightclub, so I make a fool out of myself."

Wil pulled his head back and peered at Kelsey. "If you're so in love with me, why are you dating another guy?"

"I really don't know. If you don't want me to, I won't."

"Listen to me, there's nothing between us."

She stopped and peered into his eyes. "You're so blind. Of course, there's something going on between us," she said, touching his heart. "Our hearts belong to each other." Kelsey leaned her head on his shoulder. "How long are you staying?"

"I'm not sure. Boris wants me to help him choose the next crew to go to Africa."

She looked up. "You're going, aren't you?"

"Probably, but I don't know why."

She smiled at him. "I do because that's just who you are, and that's one of the things I love about you. Please plan to spend at least one night of Christmas with me?"

"I don't know, especially since you're dating Brandon Roble. Brandon is at least ten years older than you are. What are you thinking?"

"Age has nothing to do with it when he's handsome, and besides the guy I want to be with continues to tell me there's nothing between us. Until you get your head on straight, I'll make do with other guys."

"One of these days you're going to find a guy that's perfect for you."

She looked up once more. "I have found him, but he doesn't want me."

Chapter 37

Wil blew on his gloved hands as he waited for the flight attendant, Salome, to pick him up for the Christmas party. Suddenly a pink Tesla pulled up in front of him.

"You look beautiful tonight."

She gave him a smile as she pushed the button to start the car. "Thank you. You must be pretty special to be invited to this party."

Wil looked confused. "What do you mean?"

"This party is for only the rich and important people."

"That means I'm with someone rich and important."

"Oh, heck no," Salome said. "I'm far from both, but I've always wanted to go to this party and now I have a chance. One thing you should know is I may see a guy that I'm crazy about. I'm sorry but I've had a crush on this guy for I don't know how long."

Wil grinned. "No problem, I'll step back out of the way."

"Thank you for bringing me here tonight. I owe you big time."

"You don't owe me a thing; just enjoy yourself and

don't worry about me."

After the valet took her keys, Wil and Salome walked through the doors of the auditorium which anyone who entered could tell was high class. Even Santa wore a golden suit, his reindeer were bedecked in high-class emblems, and glitter covered the tables.

Salome linked her arm with Wil's. "This is even more majestic than I thought it would be.
Could we get a drink? I'm parched."

Wil guided her to one of many bars where they stood in line behind the Lawrences.

"Well, Wil, how did you get into such a fancy get together?" Mrs. Lawrence smirked.

"I invited the two of them," Brandon said, walking up behind them. "We are the ones putting the Christmas party on after all."

"True," Mr. Lawrence said. "Where's your date for tonight?"

"Kelsey is chatting with a couple of her friends over there," Brandon said, pointing. "I'm surprised she made it tonight because she's been feeling sick the last few nights."

Mrs. Lawrence lifted an eyebrow. "Is there something we should know?"

Brandon blushed. "I'm not sure. We'll let you know as soon as we know."

"That would be wonderful news," Mr. Lawrence said. He turned to Wil. "Brandon will be the perfect son-in-law." With that, the couple ambled away without getting their drinks.

Brandon grinned. "The Lawrences have no tact whatsoever. I'm sorry you had to hear that."

"I'm happy for you if it's true."

Brandon merely said, "Enjoy your evening and Merry Christmas."

Salome tapped Wil on the shoulder. "There's my guy. I'm sorry, but he's waiting for me."

Wil stared at her. "He's with another gal."

"That's his sister. I'm going to join him. Thank you for bringing me with you and have a Merry Christmas. I wish you the best of luck with Kelsey Lawrence."

"There is nothing going on between the two of us."

Salome rolled her eyes. "Yeah, right. You aren't a particularly good liar. Anyway, enjoy yourself."

"Same to you." Wil laughed to himself as Salome hurried over to him.

Mr. Loe joined him. "You seem to lose a lot of dates."

Wil nodded. "She told me beforehand that this guy would be here. It was a way to get her in, so that's cool. Where's the missus?"

Boris pointed over to where his wife was with a group of other ladies. "They're comparing their outfits. The Christmas party tomorrow starts at noon. Don't hesitate to bring Kelsey with you."

Wil frowned. "It probably won't happen because she's dating Brandon Roble."

"Are you kidding me?"

"Nope, and it sounds like she may be pregnant."

Boris laughed. "Not likely."

"What do you mean?"

Boris patted Wil's shoulder. "The only guy Kelsey Lawrence cares about stands right next to me. The sooner you understand that, the better off you'll be."

"It'll never happen."

"Won't it? Then what is so important that you can't

take her hand and live the rest of your life with her?"

"We're not even compatible for one thing. She's rich, I'm poor. She lives in a skyscraper condo; I live in a broken-down cabin. Should I go on?"

"Even true love can break through barriers, and Kelsey Lawrence is in love with you, Wil. I'm going to pull my wife away from all those clothing fiends and enjoy a couple of dances. I'll see you tomorrow."

Wil watched as Salome and her boyfriend danced.

A voice sounded behind him. "Would you like to dance with me?"

Wil turned to Nadia. "I'd be delighted."

The two went out on the dance floor. Nadia wrapped her arms around his neck. "I'm glad you showed up. I owe you an apology from the other night."

"You don't owe me an apology."

"I do because of what I said about Kelsey. She's not as bad as I made her out to be."

"I know that."

"There is a rumor going around that she is pregnant, and Brandon is the father, which is really interesting because everyone in the Chicago social circle knows that the only guy she's been with is Nolan Gant. There is some gossip about a secret lover out of Chicago, but that could never happen because if Kelsey's father found out, he'd hit the roof and cut her out of everything. Kelsey would never want that because she's always been about the money."

Wil sighed. "I wouldn't believe everything I've heard because people like to talk."

"That's true, but most of the time it is pretty accurate. For example, everyone knows you're dating Carly Sanders. That is, everyone but your brother, Cole.

If he ever found out, he'd kill her."

"That rumor I can squelch right now because she and I aren't together. She's crazy about my brother, which I can't figure out."

Nadia grinned. "He is handsome, but then again, you're gorgeous. How would you like to see my condo?"

Wil grinned right back. "What would Kelsey think?"

She laughed. "I really don't care what Kelsey Lawrence thinks."

~

Wil grabbed a drink and watched as everyone mingled.

"What happened to your date?"

Wil turned to Kelsey who stood next to him. Wil pointed to Salome dancing with another guy. "Ten minutes after we got here, she hooked up with her boyfriend."

Kelsey laughed. "What? You can't seem to hold onto any gal. That should tell you something."

"Yeah, Salome dates this guy, and he was here at the party. She told me beforehand he'd be here and he was. Your parents and Brandon tried to 'comfort' me."

Kelsey rolled her eyes. "I can imagine how that went."

"Are congratulations in store for you?"

Kelsey's eyes widened. "What are you talking about?"

"Brandon told your parents that you've been sick. Needless to say, they're happy, and so is Brandon."

Kelsey took a deep breath. "It isn't what you think, Wil."

"I don't think anything."

"Damn you, Wilton Edgar Bolton, you should be thinking something because if I am pregnant, it would be yours and only yours. I haven't been with any man since I met you six months ago."

Wil stared at her. "You're pregnant?"

"I'm not sure. I missed my monthly cycle and have been throwing up the past couple of days. I haven't taken a pregnancy test because I don't want to know." She looked down. "That didn't come out right. I hope I'm pregnant, but we're so far apart from each other it would be just one more burden for our relationship."

He touched her hand. "It'll be okay."

She peered up at him. "How will it be okay when the man I love doesn't love me back? Tell me, Wil, how is that okay?"

"I've never said I didn't love you; I've just said we are so far apart in everything."

She glared at him, tears flowing down her face. "I don't care about any of that; I just care about you. Can't you understand that?"

Brandon walked over. "Are you okay, dear?"

Kelsey turned to him. "What are you talking about?"

"It appears you've been crying. Did Wil say something to upset you?"

"No, he hasn't done anything different than he's done in the past." Kelsey glared at Wil.

Brandon put his arm around her. "Should we dance?"

"I'd love to," Kelsey said.

Chapter 38

Wil left the social around ten-thirty and took a walk along the pier. It helped him think about everything that was going on in his mind. Of course, the main thing was Kelsey. He needed to talk to her away from everyone else.

He dialed her number, and she answered after a couple of rings. "Wil, it's almost eleven-thirty. Why are you calling?"

"I wondered if you wanted to meet me down at the pier."

"At midnight in the snow? What has gotten into you? You're not thinking clearly."

"I have a few things I need to talk to you about."

"How about you join me in my condo? I'd like to show it to you, and I promise nothing is going to happen between us. Nothing will happen until we straighten our differences out."

"Are you sure that would be okay? What about Brandon?"

"Don't worry about Brandon. I'll wait for you."

It was just after midnight when Wil knocked on Kelsey's condo door carrying a bag. She answered it dressed in a robe, took his hand, and pulled him in. "I told you this wasn't much different than what you lived in. I hope you like it."

Wil laughed. "Yeah, right. Your living room is larger than my whole cabin. And the windows have a wonderful view of Lake Michigan."

Kelsey took Wil's hand. "It is beautiful but nothing like the view of the hills, Box Elder Creek, and the wildlife wandering through the area where you live. It has always been so breathtaking to live out there. I hope to do it with you for the rest of our lives." She pulled him upstairs to her bedroom. "This is my first waterbed and I love it."

"It's a king-sized bed?"

"It is, and it's very comfortable, but you'll never set foot in it until we get our lives together."

"I hadn't planned on it," he said with a frown.

She ignored him and showed him her veranda. "This is my favorite part of the condo. A hot tub where we can soak, relax, and talk. I enjoy talking to you about anything and everything."

"In the winter?" Wil looked confused.

Kelsey grinned and pushed a button. "I can enclose it during the cold months. I would say let's hop into the hot tub together, but we both know that can't happen — at least not right now."

"I don't have a bathing suit anyway."

Kelsey waved her index finger. He followed her to a closet that she opened where he saw all of her dresses, other outfits, and some guys' suits.

He frowned. "Why would you show me men's clothes? And they're pretty fancy clothes, to boot."

Kelsey rolled her eyes. "If you think there are Brandon's or any other guy's, forget it. I know your size, and these are yours for when you need them."

"You confuse me."

"It is confusing, but deep down in my heart, I believe we will straighten out our issues, and we'll always be together. Anyway, this is my condo."

The two took the stairs and Kelsey grabbed a couple of lemonades for them. They both sat on the couch. "I'm glad you stopped by," she said. "Despite what has happened in the past few weeks, I miss you."

"I really want to change how I feel about everything, and I hope you'll help me."

"Of course, I will because I want to be in your life. I would have flown out when you called me after those deaths. Why didn't you let me?"

"Because you were with Brandon, and I didn't want to interfere with your new relationship."

"I told you I had no ties with Brandon. He is in the banking business, and it's just business. He knows your sister, Tessa, and he's ten years older than I am. Although I have nothing against older men, I prefer another guy, and that guy is you."

"What happened to you and Brandon that night?"

Kelsey laughed. "He took me to this banking business social, and guess who I should meet but your darling niece and nephew? Maddie glared at me and asked me why I was with Brandon when I should be with you."

Wil laughed. "She always liked you—even better than Lydia, and she loved her."

"It gets better. While I was talking to your niece and nephew, Brandon struck up a conversation with Tessa and the next thing I knew, he was grabbing her hand. She looked over at me and pulled her hand quickly away and hurried over to get her children. She told me she was so sorry and disappeared with them."

"What happened to Brandon?"

"We hung out for a bit longer before I told him I had a headache and wanted to go home."

Wil shook his head. "I thought the headache angle was only when you didn't want to sleep with someone."

"Silly boy, women can use it for lots of things. Now why did you come to Chicago in the first place?"

"My reason was stupid and had no chance of working out. I came to Chicago to take you back to South Dakota with me to live in the rundown cabin that I'm rebuilding, get married, have at least six children, and live a happy life with the person I genuinely love."

"Six children? Wil, that could be a dealbreaker right there."

"I'm willing to negotiate."

They both laughed, then both were silent. Wil broke the silence. "Why did you break off with your folks?"

"It was simple, and I should have done it a long time ago. I'm tired of dealing with their antics and how they manipulate people. It really hit home when they wanted to kill you in Papua New Guinea. I had my own business that was doing well, and came to find out that my dad, uncle, and Mr. Loe had all been working different angles to use it for their own gain. Then when Mr. Loe told me you had quit, I decided I was going to get away from it all too."

"Are you saying you really sold your business?"

Kelsey turned to him. "I've signed all the documents needed to sell the business to the employees, but I have thirty days to make a final decision. I want to keep the business because it's truly something I did on my own. However, if it's you or the business, I'd choose you first every time. That's what you've done to me, and no guy has ever done that. It's kind of fun actually."

"I don't want you to sell your business," Wil said, quietly.

She held his hands. "I don't want to ever lose you, and I'm serious when I say I want to have a stronger relationship with you."

"That's why I'm here. I want to start over and take it slow with you. If you agreed I thought that we'd start with a date at Loes' Christmas party tomorrow. Would you join me?"

She grinned. "That would mean I'd have to break off my engagement with my parents."

"Maybe another time."

She touched his hand. "I'll go with you, but I hope you spend part of Christmas with me."

"It is Christmas Eve, and I have a couple of things for you."

"I have nothing for you."

"Believe me, you have plenty for me. I've just been too blind to see it." He could tell Kelsey was confused. "Don't worry about it. Just open your present."

"I wondered what you had in the bag."

Kelsey tore the wrapping paper off of it and opened it. She giggled. "What is this? It looks like a combination of an antelope and a jackrabbit."

"It's a blue jackalope. A jackalope is a mythical animal of North American folklore described as a jackrabbit with antelope horns."

She reached up and kissed Wil. "This is wonderful.

I'll name him Wilton because he already reminds me of you. Thank you. What else?"

He pulled out a small gift. "Here, open this one."

She tore the wrapper and looked at the box. "Wil, you didn't, did you?"

"Just open it."

She opened it and stared at the Black Hills gold ring. "This is beautiful. I was hoping so much that it would be something else, but then it may be too soon."

Wil rolled his eyes and took the ring out of the box and put it on the pinkie of her right hand. "I've always wanted to get this for you, but the timing was always wrong."

She wrapped his arms around him and peered into his eyes. He gently pushed her hands away. "Not tonight, but soon. I promise."

Kelsey grinned. "I'll hold you to it."

Wil pulled her near him, and she melded into his chest. "Merry Christmas," he said to her.

She peered up into his eyes. "Merry Christmas to you too, dear."

Wil gently stroked her hair. "Are you missing a family Christmas celebration?"

"Not at all. You're the most important person in my life, so I'm happy to miss my family's Christmas party if it means you and I have a chance to build a better relationship." She took a sip of her drink. "Theirs are always big, extravagant get-togethers with tons of gifts no one will ever use. One year, dad gave Crystal a pair of pajamas."

"That's convenient."

Kelsey rolled her eyes. "Crystal hasn't worn pajamas in ten years. She always sleeps in the buff."

Wil's neck warmed. "I really didn't need to know that."

Kelsey laughed. "One more useless piece of info." She drew a heart on his chest. "You could join me after Mr. Loe's party."

This time Wil laughed. "I wouldn't get in the door." He stepped back. "I should get back to the hotel."

She eyed him. "You can always stay here. I do have an extra bed."

"I can't. I promised myself I want to build a relationship before the two of us ever sleep together again."

She kissed him on the cheek. "This was a particularly good start because you were able to talk to me about what's bothering you, and I could respond. We can't continue to move forward if we don't communicate with each other."

"I've figured that out. It's something new for me because my folks never communicated. I want to spend every night I can with you, but I don't want to make love with you just because it's a way to heal any wounds that we have between us."

"I thank you for that because I don't want that either. Deep in my heart, I know we'll be together, and we'll have a happy life. You'll have to find a way to forgive me for what I've done to you before that can happen."

"I told you I do forgive you."

"Your words say you forgive me, but your actions don't show that. I'll continue to tell you I'm not going anywhere, and as of this moment, I promise there will never be another guy in my life. You're it."

Chapter 39

Wil arrived at the Loes' just before noon. He was dressed in light gray jeans with a t-shirt and a blazer to match the gray jeans. He went to the bar to grab an orange juice.

Nadia was the first to greet him. "You look nice. Come with me. I want to introduce to you my mom and dad." She took his hand and pulled him over to a couple.

"Mom, Dad, this is Wil Bolton, the guy I was telling you about."

"Nice to meet you," her father said. "You're the guy who does all this treasure hunting for Boris?"

"I'm just part of the group that looks for the items."

"I understand Africa is your next destination."

Wil sipped his drink. "That's what his plans are."

The wife looked confused. "You're not going?"

"I'm not sure at this point."

Nadia smiled. "He'll go. At least that's what Leticia said."

"Your sister would know," her father said.

Wil turned and noticed Kelsey had walked in. He was just starting to approach her when Brandon walked up behind her.

Nadia followed Wil's eyes.

"Boris invited Brandon to the party because he wants to work out a deal with him on some loans. At least that's what my sister said. Does it bother you he's here?"

Wil shook his head. "No, why should it?"

"Everyone says he's sweet on Kelsey."

"That's their deal." He turned back to Nadia's parents. "It was nice meeting you two." Wil walked over to the breakfast buffet to grab some breakfast. Kelsey joined him wearing a red cashmere sweater with a printed pencil skirt that matched. Her hair was in a low French twist, and she added red lipstick.

"You look nice today."

"Thanks," she blushed. "You don't look too shabby yourself."

"I see Brandon's here."

Kelsey turned and looked toward him. "Yeah, he happened to show up at the exact time I did. He said Mr. Loe invited him to talk about a loan." She grabbed a plate and a spoonful of egg bake on it. "You didn't even ask me if we came together."

"Why would I? You told me several times I'm the only guy for you."

She smiled. "Now you're getting it."

The two grabbed a table together. "Explain to me what will happen today."

Kelsey finished chewing her egg bake. She nodded to an area of the room where a group of men and women stood. "There are a group of billionaires who show up at each other's party to make deals, gain some capital with others, and most importantly, to see all the gals." She pointed to where a bevy of females were congregated. "They are not here for sex or dating. They're more like power brokers. The real estate magnet over there and the pop singer standing in another corner can party with chief executives and dine with billionaires. In other words, the gals are leveraged to broker invitations to parties that might lead to financially enriching deals."

Wil had finished sipping his drink. "Is that what you did when you worked with your father?"

"Most of the time. See those guys standing in the shadows out of the way?"

"Yep. I'm assuming they're bodyguards."

"They are, and it's a good thing because at times it can get out of hand. There are a lot of drugs that go through these parties without anyone knowing how it happens. At least they claim they don't."

"I don't fit into any of this. Hold it, Boris asked me to invite you or said it would be okay if I brought you. Is he trying to get something out of you? If that's the case, we're out of here."

Kelsey touched Wil's arm. "That was sweet of him, but I don't think I have anything he needs."

"Then what could it be?"

"We'll just have to find out because here he comes."

"Wil, Kelsey, it's wonderful that you could make it."

"Thanks for inviting me," Wil said.

"I'm glad to see you were able to talk Kelsey into joining you."

Kelsey grinned. "He didn't have to twist my arm."

Boris laughed. "I didn't think so. Wil, I'm sure Kelsey explained how these parties work."

"She tried to explain it to me, and it's safe to say I don't fit in at all."

"Don't think for one minute you don't bring value even if you don't have as much money as we do. Like those young girls over there, you're considered capital and help us pad our coffers with funding to help with our upcoming ventures."

Wil set his plate out. "Count me out, Mr. Loe. I'm not going to be used for anyone's gain."

"You already are. I pay you a tidy sum of money to find treasures for me, and you have no problem with that."

"I'm providing a service for pay, but that's much different than what you're asking me to do."

"I'm not asking you to do anything but talk to people and answer their questions. That's it."

Kelsey jumped in. "Mr. Loe, let me talk to Wil for a moment."

He smiled at Kelsey. "I'll go mingle."

Once he was gone, Kelsey took Wil's hand, and they walked outside to the front courtyard. "I know this is a lot for you to comprehend, but it's the way people do business."

"I can't be part of that."

"What do you think is happening here?"

Wil took a deep breath. "I get it. Wow, am I stupid? Boris asked you to come because he hopes you would be able to talk me into whatever he's thinking."

Kelsey was silent for a moment.

"So much for us trying to build our relationship," Wil said. "You knew this would happen, and you didn't say anything to me about it."

"I did know the specific purpose of these events,

but I didn't know you were part of this."

He eyed her. "Don't take me for a fool. You knew exactly what was going to happen today. I'm out of here."

~

After Wil took off, Kelsey walked in and saw Mr. Loe talking to Brandon. She stormed over to the two of them.

Brandon smiled at her. "Did you straighten him out?"

She glared at both men. "You've lost Wil for good."

"What do you mean?" Mr. Loe asked.

"I mean, Wil will never trust you again, and now he thinks I'm involved with what you are doing."

"Aren't you?" Brandon asked.

"No, I'm not. I'm trying to build a relationship with the man I love, and it's been tough enough for the two of us, and now this makes it even more difficult."

Brandon laughed. "You really believe that you're going to connect with a guy who lives in a cabin in South Dakota—a man who doesn't even have a steady job?"

"It's none of your concern."

Boris jumped in. "Calm down, both of you. I have to admit I approached Wil the wrong way, but we can make this work."

"The only way you can make it work is to be upfront with him. What do you want from him?"

Boris took a deep breath. "It's simple. Treasure Paradise doesn't work if he's not involved. For some reason, the guy has a knack for finding things and making decisions on the spur of the moment. Your father and others are trying to lure him into their firms to find these items before we do."

Kelsey stared at the two of them. "I believe in Wil, but he's one person you'll never get into your fold because he doesn't trust you."

Brandon grinned. "That's where you come in."

"Me?"

"Yes," he said. "I'm sure he wouldn't want to know you had a hand in the death of Lydia Boone."

Kelsey glared at him. "How would you know something like that?"

"There's a lot of things I know about your past life. For instance, the guy in Coronado. You told Wil you didn't do anything with him, but all three of us know you spent several nights with him."

Kelsey turned red. "I'll do what I can. But the only reason I'm doing it is so he doesn't know what I've done. I'll tell him everything, but now isn't the right time."

Chapter 40

Wil sat down in the sand at the pier trying to make sense of what was happening in his life. He loved Kelsey, but he knew deep down she had a lot to do with every bad thing that had happened in his life over the past few years. Did she have anything to do with what happened to Lydia? The thought made him sick.

"This is all a lot for you to handle, and I'm sorry."

Wil peered up at Kelsey who stood over him. She slid down next to him.

"Are you okay?"

"Yeah, right. I didn't want any of this. All I wanted was to travel around the world and look for lost treasures, not be your boy toy or another rich person's 'capital,' as you've said."

Kelsey glared at him. "I told you you're not a boy toy; you're the man I truly love."

Wil glared back at her. "If that's the case, tell me the truth about the guy in Coronado. And do you know anything about what happened to Lydia?"

Kelsey's eyes widened, then she looked away. "Why would you think something like that or how would you know something like that?"

"I've just had this funny feeling that everything

that has happened you have been involved with.”

Kelsey was silent.

“That’s what I thought. You continue to tell me you want to build a relationship with me, but you can’t tell me the truth about anything.”

“What do you mean? I’ve told you a lot of things I’d never tell anyone else.”

“As long as it doesn’t interfere with what you want.”

“That’s not true, Wil, and you know it.”

“I don’t know.” He stood up and started to walk away.

“Where are you going?” she asked, jumping up.

“Back to my hotel. Tomorrow I’m flying back to South Dakota.”

Later that night, Wil was lying on his bed in the hotel room when there was a rap at his door. He opened it, and Kelsey stood there.

“You’re right, I knew about what happened to Lydia and didn’t tell you. Can I come in?”

He opened the door wider. “Why not?”

She sat down in the chair and took a deep breath. “Two years ago, I found out about you through your brother, Cole. My father and uncle had been thinking about this treasure-hunting idea for at least a year before that. Cole told them about you and your thoughts about searching for gold and treasures, and how you believed there was so much out there.

“He also told them about Lydia Boone, the girl you had fallen in love with. The idea was to find a way to get her out of your life, so you would focus on the treasures. The night she died someone told her not to drive in that car because something was going to happen to her. She didn't believe it, and then the car wreck."

Wil stared at Kelsey. "Who told her to stay out of the car?"

She wiped away a tear. "I did."

"Why didn't you go to the police?"

She stared at him. "Despite everything you think about me, I didn't ever want that to happen to Lydia. I believe in true love, and from what Cole told me, you two had that type of love."

"Thank you for trying to save her," Wil said quietly. "But you didn't go far enough. Why did you not go to the police when you first knew?"

Kelsey blew out a shaky breath. "Regrets. And there's more. I might as well tell the whole truth and nothing but the truth. I did sleep with the guy from Coronado several times, but never after I met you, and that's the truth. I'm sorry I lied to you. As for Loe and Brandon, you make your own decision on what you want you do. The only thing you need to know is that I'm in love with you. Regardless of my past, I'll always be in love with you, and I would have supported any decision you make."

"Would have?" Wil asked.

She stood up. "Yeah, I've done enough to destroy your life, so anything we had is probably pretty much over."

~

Wil caught a taxi and had the driver drop him off at the Loes' residence. The party had finished a couple of hours earlier, and it was around eight when Wil arrived. He knocked on the door, and the butler answered it and had him wait in the foyer. Boris arrived five minutes later.

"Wil, come on in."

Wil stepped in.

"I'm sorry about the way everything transpired today."

Wil laughed. "Yeah, Merry Christmas."

Boris laughed also. "No matter the situation, you always keep a good sense of humor."

"That's basically a defense mechanism."

"You came to talk? Please join me in the den, and let's have a candid talk. Lay everything out on the table."

As they entered the opulent den, Wil marveled at the large wooden desk, a table with twelve chairs around it, and large portraits of famous people on the walls. "Have a seat in one of the chairs."

They both sat down. Boris grinned. "Let's kick back and relax. They recline."

A few minutes later, the butler came in with a couple of beers. "Kelsey said you enjoyed beer."

Wil took one. "Thanks. I thought rich people preferred martinis to beer."

Boris eyed him. "Believe it or not, Kelsey got me hooked on beer. She told me this guy she really cared about loved beer. And that was before I even got to know you." He sipped his drink. "Before we start our conversation, you need to know right up front Kelsey knew nothing about what was being planned."

"But she did know about what happened to Lydia and lied to me about a couple of other things like the guy she had a liaison with in Coronado."

Boris's eyes lit up. "Wow, so she told you herself. That shows she must really love you. Brandon had tried to blackmail her by telling her he'd expose all the lies from her past to you if she didn't convince you to join us. So, she exposed all the lies herself."

"Why would Brandon do that?"

"For several reasons, I suspect. One is leverage—something rich people like to have. The other is he is in love with her. He doesn't realize that the only guy Kelsey is even remotely interested in sits in the chair right beside me."

Wil sighed. "Deep down I realize that, and every part of me wants to be with her, but I have a hard time with trust issues."

Boris nodded. "Many of us have those. The one thing I will say is you can trust Kelsey with your life. She's broken away from her family, and no one thought that would ever happen. Anyway, why are you here?"

"In the last few hours, I've thought a lot about what has been happening with my life since this treasure-hunting gig started a few months ago. I don't like being used, and you're using me to get funding."

"That's true. I should have talked to you beforehand about how all this works, but when you're rich it doesn't sound so good. But that doesn't mean I can't also learn. What do you want?"

"Simple, I want to be part of the process, and I want everything to be up-front. No more backdoor deals, and if possible, always be supportive and take care of your employees who are involved in this venture. There is so much more out there, and I want to be part of it, but I don't want the fiasco that happened in Papua New Guinea, to happen again."

"Me neither. I thought I could trust those I hired, but I didn't find out until afterward that Hank and Ben had put the screws on me. You realize the rich have ways to manipulate people anyway they can — that is all but you."

Wil sipped on his drink. "Another thing—don't lie to me. And finally, don't associate with people like Brandon, the Lawrences, and others you know are crooked."

Boris laughed. "That may be everyone I deal with in my business world, but I will do a better job to make sure that happens. The question I have for you is why should I even consider anything you have to say?"

Wil shrugged. "For some reason you believe I have this ultimate power to find things, which I don't, but like you said before, right now I have leverage."

Boris laughed once more. "You learn quickly. Come back after the first of the year, and let's put together the team."

Wil stood up. "It's a deal, but right now I have the most important thing in my life to do before it's too late."

Chapter 41

It was past eleven when Will knocked on Kelsey's door. She opened it wiping sleep out of her eyes, wearing just a t-shirt, her hair tied up in a ponytail.

"What are you doing wandering around in the middle of the night?"

"I thought maybe you would like to have a midnight chat."

She laughed. "A midnight chat? I've never heard of that."

"You realize it's cold out here."

"Join me, but remember no hanky-panky between the two of us."

"We'll see."

She grinned. "That sounds promising."

He took her hand and walked her over to the couch.

"What is up with you?"

He took a deep breath. "I just had a conversation with Boris Loe."

"Oh," Kelsey said.

"We have everything settled. I'm going on the next trip, and he's going to start telling me the truth. No more underhanded deals like tonight."

"He went for that?"

"He did."

"Good for you if that's what you want."

Wil reached into his pants pocket, pulled out a piece of paper, and handed it to Kelsey.

"What is this?"

"It's a prenuptial agreement that Maddie helped me put together. It's the first part of building a relationship. It's all there."

Kelsey laughed. "Are you kidding me?"

"Nope. All you have to do is tell me yay or nay."

"Okay, I'm game, but you're going to read me the questions."

"Fair enough."

"First, our families will never interfere in our lives."

"Yay."

"You'll never pump information out of me to use for your advantage."

Kelsey laughed. "That could be a gamebreaker, but yay."

"Next, we'll rebuild the cabin to fit our needs."

"Yay."

"Fourth, I'll require one massage a week to relax my muscles."

Kelsey laughed. "What about me?"

"I'll provide you anything you want."

"Yay, how about ironing my clothes?"

"Yay," he said.

"And cooking meals when I don't have the time?"

"Yay."

"And most important, rubbing my feet and toes after a long day of work?"

This time Wil laughed. "Yay. I just added this one.

You will never sell your business, and we'll still be together."

"Are you sure?"

"I'm positive. It's important to you, and I want to be supportive of what you do, as you are with me."

"I'll keep it. Yay." Kelsey eyed him. "I have a couple of stipulations for you. First, we spend a lot of time camping and hiking."

"Okay. Yay."

"What about a job for you? I'm not going to be the gal who supports a deadbeat husband."

Wil laughed. "I told you I'm working with Boris."

"How do I know it will be solvent?"

"You'll just have to trust me."

Kelsey stood up. "Wil, I've lied to you several times and I can see how you wouldn't trust me but I need to do something to prove to you that I'm working hard to be a better person. When we get back to South Dakota I plan to tell the sheriff everything I know about Lydia's death."

"You realize what that means."

"Yeah, I'll be testifying against my father for what he's done, my family will retaliate against me, and I'll possibly spend some time in jail. I'm terrified of spending time in jail, but I'm even more terrified of you not being in my life because I'm so in love with you."

Wil stood up and held her. "Are you sure that's what you want to do?"

She eyed Wil. "We can't live our lives together with any more lies. Anything else?"

"Finally, all-night make-out sessions once a month."

Kelsey's eyes popped out. "Just once a month?

How about once a week?"

"We can negotiate."

She took the paper from him, crumpled it up, and placed it in her pocket. "We don't need any type of prenup. How about we start our all-night make-out session right now?"

"Deal, Yay."

The next morning Wil felt Kelsey staring at him. "Didn't you sleep?"

"No way, not after last night. That was a perfect evening between the two of us. I'm glad we were able to talk about where we're heading. We have a long way to go, but it's a start, and I feel good about that." She rolled over on top of him and kissed him. "We have one more thing to do before you leave." Kelsey rolled off him, slipped into a t-shirt, and hurried into the bathroom. She came out with a packet and sat beside Wil. "Remember when Brandon and my family told you I could be pregnant?"

Wil grinned at her. "There is a rumor going around that you have a secret lover outside of Chicago."

She kissed him. "That's not a rumor; that's a true statement. Right now, we're going to find out if you're going to be a father." Kelsey went to take the test, and the two waited to see what happened.

When the color appeared, she said, "I'm sorry."

THE END

Other books by this author

Bouncing Back

The Battle Off the Court

Success on the Hard Wood

Tragedy Off the Court

Freedom Flight

Fight for Survival

Road to Hell

A New Life Begins

Relentless

Missing

Targeted

Author Bio: My wife, Susan and I have two sons, Justin (Kayla) and Jeremy and a grandson, Aiden. Born and raised in South Dakota. I enjoy spending time with family, traveling and putt-putt. I recently retired as managing editor of a small town Iowa newspaper. I am a former Marine Corps veteran, getting my start in the publishing business in 1981 working for several years on base newspapers. I spent time running my own freelance business. I love writing. I enjoy reading anything and everything. I also love the history of our country and enjoy reading western books, mysteries, and adventure novels, and watching mystery, adventure, and western movies.

www.ingramcontent.com/pod-product-compliance
Lightning Source LLC
Chambersburg PA
CBHW060314310726
48976CB00007B/2321